EVERY SECOND
THURSDAY

'The suspense never flags . . . distinctly high-class entertainment'
Kirkus Reviews

'A very sound and satisfying performance'
Financial Times

'Ingenious, slow-burn tale . . . easy, readable prose'
The Times

EVERY SECOND THURSDAY

Emma Page

KEYHOLE CRIME
London · Sydney

First published in Great Britain 1981 by
William Collins Sons & Co. Ltd

Copyright © Emma Page, 1981

Australian copyright 1982

This edition published 1982 by
Keyhole Crime, 15–16 Brook's Mews,
London W1A 1DR

ISBN 0 263 73978 3

06/0882

Made and printed in Great Britain by
Cox & Wyman Ltd, Reading

For Christopher
with love

CHAPTER 1

Eight o'clock on a clear golden morning in late September. The village of Abberley had been awake and astir for an hour or more. On the road that led north out of the village to the town of Cannonbridge two miles away, a tall house named Lynwood stood up on a bank and looked west across the valley. It was a substantial dwelling of graceful proportions, dating back to the early years of Victoria's reign, set on the edge of farmland with smooth lawns falling away from it on all sides.

In the large front bedroom on the first floor Vera Foster settled back into the nest of lacy pillows that Miss Jordan had just shaken up with professional efficiency.

Vera ate the last of her porridge, beautiful thick creamy porridge cooked all night in the kitchen Aga in the Scottish fashion. Her father—now dead—had been Scottish. That was how he liked his porridge cooked, that was how it continued to be cooked at Lynwood, nine years after his death.

Very gingerly she moved her left leg into a better position. The sciatica was receding now but regular attacks over the last few years had taught her a wary respect for the pain and its ability to spring suddenly back at her when she had fancied it vanquished.

Over by the long windows Miss Jordan drew the rose-flowered curtains further apart.

'It's a lovely morning,' she said in her precise tones. 'I'm sure it's going to turn out warm this afternoon. I could move a chair out on to the balcony. If you wrapped up you could sit out for half an hour.'

'I'm certainly not well enough to sit outside,' Vera said crossly. A stubborn look appeared in her china-blue eyes.

She drank her coffee with a moody air.

The sciatica laid her low with relentless regularity twice a year, in spring and autumn. She made the most of these enforced retreats, expecting — and receiving — a good deal of pampering and cossetting.

But Miss Jordan was a newcomer to Lynwood; she had been sent by the Cannonbridge agency a couple of weeks ago in response to an urgent request from Vera. She was not a trained nurse but a companion help with some nursing experience. She was a tall angular woman in her early forties with a sharp-featured face and a disciplined, authoritative manner. She adopted towards her patient a more bracing attitude than Vera was accustomed to. Competent and careful Miss Jordan certainly was, attentive enough, even kind in her impersonal way, but indulgent and cossetting she certainly was not.

Vera had attempted at the start of the fortnight to address Miss Jordan by her first name — which was Edith — but Miss Jordan was by no means disposed to allow such familiarity. She had never done so, never considered it wise, certainly didn't intend to begin now. Had she permitted it, Mrs Foster would very shortly in return have asked her to call her Vera, in the hope of establishing the kind of indulgent cosy intimacy she had known with her father and had been ceaselessly trying to find elsewhere ever since his death.

Vera's father, Duncan Murdoch, was over seventy when he died and he had been in declining health for several months. But his death had all the same struck his daughter a shattering blow.

He had been working in his study on the ground floor of Lynwood — he ran his own business, the Cannonbridge Thrift Society, and he used the Lynwood study as a subsidiary office in addition to his regular office in the town.

Vera had just looked in to see if her father wanted coffee. He glanced up and smiled at her with his usual

look of affection. He said, 'That would be a very good —'
and suddenly clutched at his chest and fell forward across
the desk.

He was dead from a massive heart attack before Doctor
Tredgold arrived eight minutes later, snatched from the
middle of morning surgery.

But that was all nine years ago, when Vera was still a
pretty young woman, certainly a total stranger to the
sciatica that afflicted her these days. Now she settled
herself further back against the pillows and levelled a
mulish look at Miss Jordan's straight and elegant back.

'I have no intention of stirring from this bed for
another week,' she said in a louder tone than was
necessary. 'I'm sure Doctor Tredgold doesn't expect me to
get up so soon.'

Miss Jordan turned from the window. Her neat overall
covered a tailored dress cut on classic lines. She wasn't
good-looking but there was something in her calm face
that drew the eye.

Her delicate skin had a pale, creamy tint and she wore
no make-up. She had a good deal of thick dark hair
arrestingly streaked with white; it was drawn back into a
heavy knot at the nape of her neck. Her eyes, a light clear
hazel, were large and well set.

'Oh, come now, Mrs Foster,' she said in a rallying tone.
'I'm sure Doctor Tredgold expects better results than that
from his treatment. When he was here on Monday he told
me I wouldn't be needed here much longer.' Miss Jordan
went out from the Cannonbridge agency on short-term
postings. 'He thought I'd be able to leave early next
week.'

'You can't possibly leave as soon as that,' Vera said in
loud protest. 'I won't hear of it.'

There was a sound of movement along the corridor,
footsteps in the adjoining bedroom. Vera glanced towards
the connecting door. It opened a little and her husband's

face appeared in the aperture.

'Just seeing to my overnight bag,' he said with amiable briskness. 'I'll be with you in a moment.' His face vanished from the doorway.

Vera drew a long sighing breath. 'I've finished with the tray,' she said abruptly to Miss Jordan. 'I'll do my hair now.'

Miss Jordan removed the tray and brought some toilet articles over from the dressing-table. She set them down within Vera's reach.

Miss Jordan had very smooth white-skinned hands with long slim fingers. She did a good deal of fine needlework and took great care of her hands.

She held the mirror while Vera teased the front of her hair into artless curls. Her hair had always been fine and delicate and was now growing perceptibly thinner. The colour, once a soft honey-blonde, was now harsher and deeper from regular tinting. The sciatica had prevented her from visiting the hairdresser in Cannonbridge and greyish streaks showed along her temples and parting.

'My make-up tray,' she commanded and Miss Jordan brought across the lipstick and powder, the eye-shadow and mascara.

'Are you good with hair?' Vera asked as she worked on her face. Perhaps Miss Jordan could wash her hair with a colour shampoo; it might serve as temporary concealment for the grey. 'Today's Thursday,' she added. 'Alma could buy a shampoo for me this afternoon in Cannonbridge.' Alma Driscoll was the Lynwood housekeeper. Every Thursday she set off from Lynwood after lunch for a jaunt into Cannonbridge.

Each alternate week Alma didn't return to Lynwood till next morning, spending the night at another house in Abberley village, an Edwardian villa called Pinetrees, standing about a quarter of a mile from Lynwood.

Pinetrees belonged to a couple who had been friends of

Vera Foster's father. They were both old now and frail, very dependent on the services of their resident housekeeper. Once a fortnight this housekeeper went off to see her married daughter in a neighbouring village. She spent the night there and caught the first bus back in the morning. By arrangement with Vera, Alma Driscoll stayed the night at Pinetrees in her place, to keep a friendly eye on the old couple.

'If Alma gets me the shampoo,' Vera went on, 'do you think you could wash my hair tomorrow?'

'Certainly.' Miss Jordan had spent nearly ten years in one post — before she took up temporary work with the agency — and she had washed and waved the long white tresses of that fastidious employer on a great many occasions. She could certainly cope with Mrs Foster's scanty locks.

Vera patted turquoise eye-shadow — too lavish and too bright — over her crêpy lids. 'If you didn't know how old I was,' she said suddenly, 'what age would you take me for?' She stared intently at her reflection in the mirror. 'Be honest, I shan't be offended.'

She had told Miss Jordan at their first encounter that she was thirty-two. In fact she was forty and looked fifty. She cherished the illusion that Miss Jordan was about to reply twenty-eight. Or thirty at the very most.

Miss Jordan knew well what Mrs Foster wished to hear. 'Twenty-nine,' she said judicially, splitting the difference.

Vera's expression softened. She made a pleased inclination of her head and for a moment Miss Jordan could see the girl she once had been, Daddy's little darling, pretty, cherished. And hopelessly spoiled.

Vera brushed mascara — too thick and too dark — over her sparse lashes. 'I've been married for eight years now, believe it or not,' she said with a complacent air.

'Indeed.' Miss Jordan had no difficulty in crediting the eight years, she could have swallowed eighteen without demur.

'I take it you've never been married?' Vera asked.

'I have not.'

'You've never felt the need?' Vera persisted with unlovely curiosity.

'I most certainly have not.' Miss Jordan's lips came together in a grim line. 'Nor am I likely to.'

'Oh, you never know,' Vera said lightly.

'Indeed I do know,' Miss Jordan said with force. 'One does not marry by accident.'

The connecting door opened wide and Gerald Foster came into the room.

'I think I've got everything,' he said cheerfully. 'I'll be off in a few minutes.' He advanced towards the bed, smiling at his wife.

He was a little above average height, with a spare figure and narrow shoulders. He was six years younger than Vera but looked considerably older than his age, not because of any greying or fading but from the many lines on his face. His habitual expression was of reflection and calculation, of devoting sustained and intense thought to the complicated business of living.

He had never really looked young, not even as a lad, he had always looked like a serious adult temporarily inhabiting the skin and flesh of a child — a boy — a youth.

Eight years ago when he and Vera got married, with Vera at thirty-two briefly restored by the stimulus of the event to the pretty flush of youth, and Gerald at twenty-six looking even more solemn and unsmiling under the weight of his new responsibilities, anyone would have taken Vera for the younger of the pair. Now they seemed much of an age, somewhere in the vague stretches of middle life.

'I'll phone you about nine o'clock this evening,' Gerald said. 'Just to see that everything's all right.' He patted his wife's hand with an affectionate smile.

Miss Jordan turned from the bedside and made to leave

the room discreetly, but Vera raised a hand to halt her.

'There's no need to go rushing off,' she said. 'You can clear away these things.'

Miss Jordan gave a little nod and busied herself gathering up the toilet articles while contriving with professional ease to efface herself from the presence of the married couple and whatever private conversation they might be about to engage in.

'I'll try not to be late back tomorrow,' Gerald said. 'With luck I should be here by seven or eight.'

He was off on a business trip to Lowesmoor, a large town some seventy miles away. He had worked as a clerk for Vera's father, had been highly thought of by that shrewd gentleman. After Murdoch's death Gerald had taken charge of the business; he had gone in for a programme of systematic expansion and made a considerable success of it.

'I wish you didn't have to go away,' Vera said with a pout that had ceased to be girlishly attractive a good ten years ago but which she mistakenly retained in her armoury. 'You know I hate it here on my own.'

'I go away as little as I can,' Gerald said with an air of great reasonableness. 'Hardly ever for more than one night and never more than twice in a month.' He smiled. 'You don't want me to neglect the business, do you?'

'All this expansion,' Vera said mutinously. 'I can't see it's necessary. I'm sure Daddy would have thought it risky.'

He gave her a humouring smile. 'I never take unnecessary risks, my dear, you know that.'

She wasn't to be won over so easily. 'Daddy didn't find it necessary to keep going away. He hardly ever went away on business.'

She led a very shut-in life. She had no close women friends, no relatives, scarcely any visitors. She had been very close to her father, had been desolated by his death, had tried to replace him with Gerald, not altogether with the success for which she strove and was still striving.

He stooped and kissed her cheek. 'I'll get my things,' he said, 'then I must be off.' As he turned towards the connecting door he added mildly, 'Times have changed a good deal since your father's day. The business is very different now.'

Indeed it was. Duncan Murdoch had been the grandson of a Scottish crofter. His father had left the croft as a young man and gone south, to England, in search of lusher pastures. He worked for some years as a clerk, living with the utmost frugality, saving every penny. He laid out this little capital by way of small weekly loans to workmates spent up before pay-day.

Eventually he left paid employment and started a thrift and credit-voucher business of his own. The little enterprise prospered. He never overreached himself, was content with a modest success.

His son Duncan worked as his assistant, inheriting the business on his father's death. He broadened its scope to include hire purchase and various other kinds of minor financial transactions. He kept it all on a very sound and stable footing; indeed, his temperament and upbringing made him excessively cautious. He was never gifted with imagination or business vision.

On his death the business passed to Vera, his only child. She would have been incapable of running it on her own and was greatly relieved when Gerald Foster — at that time her father's clerk — agreed to take over the running.

Six months later they were married and became joint owners, joint partners in the enterprise. In actual practice this meant that Gerald continued to run the business and at regular intervals placed a sheaf of papers before his wife for her signature.

Duncan Murdoch had kept a lot of good capital locked up, earning its safe little percentage, risking nothing, producing nothing. Gerald Foster knew the value of capital from never having been able to lay his hands on any. He had inherited nothing from his poverty-stricken parents.

In his clerking days he had saved every penny, done what he could with it, but it never amounted to a row of beans.

As soon as he found himself in control of the Cannon-bridge Thrift Society he lost no time in putting Duncan Murdoch's reserve capital to work, shrewdly and carefully.

He kept all the original basis of the business but branched out to embrace small property deals, very small to begin with, tail-end bargains from executors' sales and the like, run-down shops, clapped-out businesses, disreputable-looking cottages.

Everything he touched prospered. The cottages cleaned up and modernized remarkably well, the shops sold to developers who pulled them down and reared in their place neat modern frontages.

And Foster was above all fortunate in being able to jump on the bandwagon at the right time. When the markets took a tumble and inflation ran riot, he was busy buying and selling, trading and dealing.

But he didn't lose his head, didn't start to fancy himself a potential tycoon. He had the little office in Cannon-bridge done up and made a good deal more efficient and convenient. But that was all.

He employed only one assistant, a general clerk. She was a formidably competent and respectable woman of powerful build and indeterminate age. He would no more have dreamed of employing some daft and decorative little eye-catcher unschooled in letters and numbers than his father-in-law would have done.

Foster came back now into his wife's bedroom carrying a briefcase and an overnight bag. 'You're certainly looking a lot better,' he said bracingly. 'You should be up in a day or two.'

'I feel very far from well,' Vera said with one of her sudden fits of moodiness. 'You have no idea how painful sciatica can be.'

'I don't suppose I have,' he said with an air of apology. He stooped and kissed her cheek. 'But I do know I'm leaving you in very good hands.'

He gave a little formal nod in the direction of Miss Jordan, who made a vestigial bow in return, to indicate that she had heard and appreciated the compliment, while still contriving to remain invisible—and indeed absent from the scene.

'It's so boring,' Vera said fretfully. 'Stuck here all day with nothing to do.'

'You can surely find something to entertain you.' Gerald waved a hand at the television set, the radio, books, magazines. 'If there's anything else you want, I'm sure Miss Jordan or Alma will be happy to get it for you.' Vera moved her head sulkily but made no reply.

He patted her shoulder. 'Do cheer up, my dear. It's a lovely day.' He picked up his cases. 'I must be off, I have to call in at the office first. Miss Greatbach will be wondering where I've got to.' He smiled again and was gone before Vera might decide to allow tears to trickle down her cheeks.

Downstairs in the kitchen the housekeeper, Alma Driscoll, was busy with her chores and at the same time chatting amiably to her uncle, Matt Bateman. Matt was sitting at the table, finishing off the substantial snack-meal Alma had set before him.

He was a retired labourer living alone in a tiny cottage half a mile along the road to Abberley village. He had never married, had never seen much good come of it, nothing but loss of freedom and general aggravation. He dropped in at the Lynwood kitchen most days, to see his niece, drink a cup of tea, have a bite to eat. And cast his sharp eye round for any little unwanted trifles that might be doing nobody any good just lying about, but might come in very handy at his little cottage.

Alma rinsed out the teapot and set it down on a shelf. The room was large, with what had once been a butler's pantry opening off it.

Vera's parents had had the house modernized when they moved into it immediately after their marriage. Gerald Foster had caused further substantial improvements to be carried out after his own marriage. Vera would have been quite happy if he had left the house as it was; she would have felt that this enshrined her father's memory.

But she was pleased all the same when the improvements were carried out. She appreciated the new comfort and convenience even if her nature didn't allow her to open her mouth and say so.

Alma picked up the teacups from the table and carried them to the sink. She was a plump, cheerful-looking woman in her middle thirties. She had married once and lived to regret it. She was now a resolute divorcée amusing herself when and where she chose.

She glanced up at the clock. 'Time you were taking yourself off,' she said to her uncle with pleasant firmness.

He got to his feet. There was one further benefit from his visit that he intended to have.

'I'll just have a word with the gaffer,' he said easily. 'About the firewood.' There was a beautiful lot of wood lying along the edge of the Lynwood shrubbery where the jobbing gardener, Ned Pritchard, had piled it two days ago.

Matt had marked the wood for his own. It would burn very nicely in the kitchen of his little cottage.

'You certainly will not ask Mr Foster about the firewood,' Alma said. 'I won't have any kin of mine coming here cadging.'

She saw nothing amiss in diverting a certain amount of Mr Foster's food and drink towards her uncle in the course of his frequent calls at Lynwood. That was straightforward perks and nothing to be ashamed of.

And she made no secret of the pie or spiced fruit-loaf that she carried in her basket when she called in at Matt's cottage. But that was quite definitely as far as she would go.

'Miss Vera wouldn't mind if I had the wood,' Matt said. 'Her Dad would have let me have it if he was still alive. A fine old gentleman, Mr Murdoch, I always got on well with him.'

'And Mr Foster's a first-class employer,' Alma retorted. 'I get on well with him. And I mean to keep on getting on well with him. You're not asking him for that wood.'

'Ned Pritchard'll have it if I don't,' Matt said with resigned protest.

'That's up to Mr Foster. It's his wood, he can do what he pleases with it.'

Matt pulled on his jacket with its deep and well-used pockets not immediately visible to the questioning eye. He picked up his cup.

'Now mind,' Alma said as he opened the door. 'One word about that wood and you'll have me to reckon with.'

'I shan't say anything.' He'd already set his mind on another and equally fertile source of free fuel. No need to mention the fact to Alma. She was a dear girl but she did go on a bit.

'You'll be looking in at the cottage this afternoon?' he asked.

She gave a nod. 'I'll see you as usual.'

'This is your night for sleeping out at Pinetrees?'

'That's right.' She came out of the kitchen and stood beside him on the doorstep, looking out at the mellow day.

'It's a lovely time of year,' Matt said with deep pleasure. 'The pheasants will be fine and fat now.'

She gave him a sharp slap on the arm. 'Don't let me hear of you poaching,' she said fiercely.

Not that he'd ever actually been hauled up into court and charged with poaching, and not that he'd ever admitted such an activity to her, but she had grave suspicions all the same. He gave her a reassuring grin and she turned back into the kitchen.

Matt walked along the side of the house and saw Mr Foster backing his car out of the garage. Matt couldn't help himself, he took a chance; no need for Alma to know if it didn't come off. He went up to the car and stooped by the window.

'All right if I take that bit of wood?' he said amiably to Mr Foster. 'I'll give you an hour or two in the garden for it.'

Gerald Foster turned from his own preoccupations and was momentarily irritated by the cheerful cadginess of Bateman, Matt's happy assumption that other men strove so that he could help himself to the fruits of their labours.

At another time Gerald might easily have nodded agreement, might have been no more than mildly amused by Bateman's cheek. But now he said curtly, 'It's certainly not all right. You leave that wood where it is. Ned Pritchard is to have it. He chopped it down.' Gerald began to turn his car.

'That's all right, Mr Foster,' Matt said genially. 'No offence intended and none taken, I hope.' Gerald merely nodded and grunted in reply and Matt went swinging off down the drive.

He whistled as he strode along the road. He walked with a strong upright carriage, jaunty and free. He was still agile and quick on his feet in spite of his sixty-nine years.

All his life he'd been a country lad, wouldn't give you

tuppence for the town. He disapproved of almost every change that had taken place in his lifetime. He ignored the greater part of those changes and lived his life in a manner not much different from the way his father had lived his.

Matt lived in the cottage where he had been born; during his working life he'd been a labourer in the local quarry where his father and grandfather had worked before him.

In Matt's eyes the village of Abberley was the centre of the universe. He'd grown up with the strong conviction—passed on to him from his father—that disaster would surely strike any man rash enough to wander far from his native sod.

He had set foot in the neighbouring town of Cannonbridge no more than a couple of dozen times in his life. He'd been further afield than that only once, in the days when his Dad was alive.

The Vicar had organized a coach outing to the seaside on the occasion of the Silver Jubilee of King George the Fifth. Matt's Dad had prophesied disaster for the outing, and Matt's Dad had been right.

Matt was sick on the coach going to the sea and even more sick on the coach coming back. As he finally staggered off the coach at the end of the day he vowed never again to set foot on anything more venturesome than the bus into Cannonbridge.

He glanced about him now as he swung along. I'll slip on up to Farmer Jauncey's top field, he decided. Plenty of good wood up there and Jauncey didn't mind him slipping along once in a way to help himself.

Matt was as vigilant and observant as any professional gamekeeper and in return for the blind eye turned on his own pursuits by local landowners he made sure no gangs of townee villains came on to their terrain to plunder and steal in quantities Matt couldn't and wouldn't have shifted in a dozen lifetimes of semi-honest endeavour.

He reached the top field and surveyed the ground. He would just take enough wood now to be going on with, he could come back again later.

His sharp eyes spotted some droppings under a tree and he stood for a minute or two staring up into the branches with keen interest.

Then he pulled a length of stout rope from one of his pockets and began to pile up a nice selection of boughs, ready to sling the bundle across his shoulders.

It was still not quite ten o'clock. Miss Jordan went quietly up from the kitchen where she had been drinking coffee with Alma and softly opened the door of Mrs Foster's bedroom.

She peeped in to see if Mrs Foster was settling down for her nap. But Vera was still wakeful; she heard the whisper of the door.

'I'm not asleep,' she said loudly. 'Come in.'

Miss Jordan went into the room. 'Would you like your hot chocolate now?' she asked. Vera was very fond of hot sweet drinks, chocolate in particular.

'No, I'll have it later. I want you to phone Doctor Tredgold now, I don't feel at all well.'

Miss Jordan glanced at her watch. 'You must phone him right away,' Vera insisted. The doctor was a stickler about time. He liked all house calls to be notified before ten o'clock.

'I can't in all honesty tell him,' Miss Jordan said with a small sigh, 'that I think he ought to call. I can't see that you need him. He's a very busy man.'

Tredgold was no longer young and his temper wasn't sweetening with advancing years. But Vera wouldn't dream of changing doctors. He'd been her father's doctor, her own doctor since she was a child of seven.

She began to struggle up in the bed. 'If you don't phone

him, then I will,' she said with determination.

'Very well, I'll do as you ask.' But Miss Jordan wouldn't make use of the phone beside the bed. She was far too professional for such amateur indiscretions. She went down to the study; the phone there wasn't connected to the one in the bedroom.

A few minutes later she went back up the stairs, carrying a tray. 'Doctor Tredgold will be here about half past eleven,' she told Mrs Foster.

She set down the cup of chocolate and a small plate of the sugary biscuits Mrs. Foster liked. She made no mention of the doctor's irritated references to neurotic female patients and the wasting of his valuable time.

'I knew he'd come,' Vera said with a satisfied smile. 'He always comes when I want him.' She waved a hand. 'I'll have the white tablets now.'

Miss Jordan brought over the bottle; it was almost empty. Vera tipped a tablet out into her palm. 'I'll have to ask him for some more of these,' she said.

As she sipped her chocolate she suddenly said, 'You might pass me my father's photograph.'

This was a large studio portrait. Vera often liked to hold it, to look at her father's wide brow and resolute chin, letting the happy days of the past rise up before her.

Miss Jordan picked up the photograph in its heavy silver frame and carried it over to the bed.

'I've always liked this one best,' Vera said fondly. She smiled down at her father, sitting with one hand propped under his chin, gazing back at her with his shrewd and penetrating look.

'That's the way I remember Daddy. Sitting at his desk downstairs, looking just like that, thinking about things.'

CHAPTER 2

It was past noon by the time Doctor Tredgold's car halted outside the front door of Lynwood.

'Mrs Foster can be very difficult when she chooses,' the doctor said to Miss Jordan as they went up the stairs. 'But I'm sure there's no need for me to tell you not to pamper her.' He had formed a high regard for Miss Jordan's competence.

'Mrs Foster's very much inclined to make the most of this sciatica,' he added. 'Nothing she likes better than being waited on and fussed over.' A widower now for many years, with his own burden of aches and pains to bear as the years ground remorselessly on, he had less and less sympathy these days with any attitude on the part of his patients that remotely resembled hypochondria.

'I've already mentioned that I'm thinking of leaving in a few days,' Miss Jordan said.

He nodded energetically. 'That's the ticket. Force her to get up. She'd stay in bed till Christmas if we let her.'

They reached the door of Vera's bedroom. 'Come now,' Tredgold said to his patient with forceful joviality as soon as Miss Jordan showed him into the room. 'Why aren't you sitting outside on this beautiful day?' Vera made no reply; her face took on a mutinous look.

The curtains were partly drawn together against the dazzling sunlight and the doctor crossed to the window and drew them fully apart. He glanced out at the valley lying tranquil in the sparkling air.

'We won't get many more days like this before winter,' he said. 'You should make the most of them.'

Miss Jordan withdrew to the door. 'I'll be just along the corridor if you should need me,' she said as she went out and closed the door behind her.

The doctor stood looking out at the hill opposite, at the porcupine crest of trees along the ridge, the green tints shading from palest lime to deepest olive.

'I've always loved that view.' He was silent for a moment, remembering how he had stood there in Duncan Murdoch's time; Duncan had been a valued friend. He gave a little sigh and turned back to the bed with a softer expression.

'Is the leg really painful still?' he asked with a little grin. 'Or are you laying it on—just a bit?'

Vera closed her eyes. 'The pain comes and goes. It's still pretty bad at times.' She opened her eyes. 'I need some more of the white tablets.'

He picked up the bottle and looked at the few remaining tablets. 'You're taking a lot of these,' he said with mild reproof. 'You should take them only when you find it necessary, not three times a day like clockwork.'

She pulled a little face, placatory, like a child. 'I don't take them as often as that. But you can see I need some more, they're almost finished.'

He gave her a considering glance. She returned his gaze. Her expression changed to a bolder, defiant stare. 'I'm not a baby,' she said with spirit.

His eyes held hers for a few seconds, then he shrugged. 'Oh, very well.'

Irritability rose inside him but he pushed it sternly down. He had two more calls to make before lunch and already he felt worn out. 'You can get Alma to call in for the tablets this afternoon.' He pulled out a pad and began to write.

'It's Alma's day for Cannonbridge,' Vera said. 'She won't be back here till tomorrow morning. This is the night she sleeps at Pinetrees.'

'Oh, yes.' It was at Tredgold's suggestion that Vera had offered the old couple at Pinetrees this use of Alma's services. 'It's very good of you to let her go there,' he said. 'I know they appreciate it.'

He leaned down and patted her hand, gave her a little indulgent smile, remembering her all at once as a child with long fair pigtails and bright blue eyes, running up to him, laughing, catching at his hand.

'Take your time,' he said, against the judgment of his professional nature. 'If you want to take it easy for another day or two, stay where you are.'

He looked at his watch. 'You can ask Miss Jordan to call in for the tablets. Any time after four.'

The kitchen clock struck two. 'You go and get yourself ready,' Miss Jordan said to Alma Driscoll. 'I'll finish the washing-up for you.' She smiled and her face at once looked younger and less sombre, almost handsome. 'You can trust me to do it properly,' she added lightly. 'I've done it often enough in my life.'

Alma unfastened her vast gingham apron and turned from the sink. 'Oh, that is kind of you,' she said with eager acceptance. She hung the apron up behind the door and dried her hands on the roller towel. 'I do appreciate it.'

She'd come across more than one temporary lady help from staff agencies. Half of them couldn't wash a teacup and the other half wouldn't dream of lowering themselves by attempting it.

Miss Jordan picked up a pair of rubber gloves and smoothed them on. 'It really is nothing,' she said as she ran fresh hot water into the basin.

'Don't forget Mrs Foster's porridge,' Alma reminded her. Though she was sure Miss Jordan didn't really need reminding, she'd made the porridge very nicely the last time Alma had slept out at Pinetrees.

'No, I won't forget. You go off and enjoy yourself, don't worry about a thing.' Miss Jordan began to wash the dishes.

Alma hurried up the back staircase to her comfortable bedroom at the rear of the house. She performed a swift but careful toilet.

I'll be quite sorry to see Miss Jordan leave when Mrs Foster's downstairs again, she thought as she sat at her dressing-table, arranging her curly auburn hair into its most becoming style. Miss Jordan was very efficient but she didn't put your back up like some did by making a song and dance about her efficiency.

And she was happy to take her meals in the kitchen with Alma, none of that irritating nonsense of having to lay a single place in the dining-room or run about after her with dainty trays. What was more, she managed to be companionable without being either inquisitive or secretive.

Alma pulled on her tweed coat. No need for a hat today, thank goodness, nice and warm, no breeze to speak of. She was proud of her abundant springing hair and never covered it up without good cause.

She gave herself a comprehensive glance in the long mirror of the wardrobe. Not bad for thirty-five, you could see many worse in a day's march.

She picked up her handbag and went gaily off down the stairs and into the kitchen to pick up the basket she had put ready earlier.

'Have a good time,' Miss Jordan said with a friendly smile.

'I certainly will.' Alma went out through the side door into the sweet-smelling afternoon.

She shifted the basket into a comfortable position on her arm. As well as her library books the basket held some socks and vests she had laundered for her uncle, a wedge of dark moist fruit-cake and an apple pie just the way he liked it, sweet and juicy, with a hint of cinnamon.

Alma and her uncle got on very well. Matt was her mother's older brother. Alma had never had any father worth mentioning, she had only the vaguest idea of who he might have been and didn't greatly care. It had never seemed to bother her mother and Alma saw little reason why it should bother her.

Her mother had died in middle life from some sudden and furious disease of the blood, at just about the time when Alma had come to the end of her own disastrous foray into matrimony.

In the general upheaval and desolation Alma had arrived on her uncle's doorstep. He took her in, was very good to her in those wretched weeks, and she never forgot it.

Matt had done odd jobs up at Lynwood ever since he was a lad and it was he who suggested the Lynwood job to Alma. It was not long after Gerald Foster's marriage to Vera, and Matt knew that Mr Foster was looking for someone to help in the house.

In Duncan Murdoch's day the Lynwood kitchen had been ruled over by Hetty Attwood, an old-fashioned and increasingly eccentric domestic who had originally been engaged by his wife when they were first married.

Mrs Murdoch didn't survive the birth of Vera and in the bleak time that followed, Hetty Attwood was utterly indispensable to Duncan Murdoch. He would never have dreamed of repaying her by sending her packing in her declining and deteriorating years.

Gerald Foster well knew the domestic situation at Lynwood long before he married Vera; in the course of his work for Murdoch he was often in the house. He was well aware that Hetty Attwood was not only far from competent but also by no means completely honest in her household dealings.

Vera turned a blind eye to these shortcomings — Hetty had been her father's servant and, before that, the servant of her parents, and so must not be judged by ordinary standards.

But these sentiments weighed not at all with Gerald. He intended to get rid of Hetty as soon as he could decently manage it after moving into Lynwood as master of the house.

As a first step he set about finding a replacement for Hetty. Matt Bateman mentioned that his niece, young, energetic and competent, was looking for a post.

Gerald managed to persuade Vera that they should take Alma on to assist Hetty, but he couldn't prevail on her to give Hetty her marching orders.

It was a good seven years after Alma Driscoll first stepped over the Lynwood threshold before Gerald finally managed to bid goodbye to Hetty—with a suitable and indeed generous financial provision, in recognition of her long service.

Alma now reigned over the Lynwood household. If extra help was needed it was brought in temporarily and with her agreement. She was well satisfied with her present situation.

She hummed a tune as she walked briskly along the road towards her uncle's cottage. She reached Matt's gate and walked up the neat path between trim flower-borders to the front door. She turned the handle and went in. Half an hour's pleasant chat with her uncle, leaving in good time to catch the bus outside the pub on the village green.

Three quarters of an hour later she stepped on board the bus. She settled back luxuriously into her seat at the rear.

She looked forward with pleasure to her outing. A ten-minute ride would deposit her in the centre of Cannonbridge, bustling and lively on market day. A good prowl round the shops—mustn't forget Mrs Foster's colour shampoo, light golden blonde.

Pity Mrs Foster was going grey so early, she'd had such pretty soft pale hair when Alma first saw her—must be

eight years or more now, she calculated with fleeting surprise at the swift passage of the years.

After the shopping, a long browse in the public library,
stocking up with the historical romances she loved. Then
she would call in, as she did every Thursday, at a little
terrace house in an Edwardian crescent behind the
library, to have a substantial high tea with Rosie Trewin,
a friend she had known for some years. Rosie used to work
at the pub by the green in Abberley, but she'd left a
couple of years ago to marry a Cannonbridge man; they
now had a six-month-old baby.

Alma opened her handbag and took out a fruit pastille;
she popped it into her mouth. At the prospect of the
afternoon and evening before her she sighed with
pleasure. What more could anyone reasonably ask?

Seventy miles away in Lowesmoor a church clock struck
three quarters. Gerald Foster paused for a moment and
glanced at his watch, then he resumed his careful pacing
of the building site, the third of four he had driven over to
see.

He always inspected and assessed on his own, couldn't
tolerate an agent at his heels, interfering with the keen
flow of calculation through his brain.

Gerald considered Lowesmoor a vigorous, thrusting
town, poised for expansion, definitely a place to invest in.
He left the site and climbed a small eminence nearby in
order to view the terrain from above. No insoluble problems, no difficulties with access, altogether satisfactory.

He went back to his car and drove slowly about the
district, gauging the tone and character of the neigh-
bourhood. When he was satisfied, he found a phone kiosk
and rang the agent's office. It was now almost half past
five.

'I'm ready to talk terms,' he told the agent. 'What
about dinner at my hotel this evening?' Tomorrow was

already mapped out and Gerald wasn't a man to watch with any pleasure the long hours of evening slip unprofitably away in idle recreation.

'Good idea,' the agent said, and they arranged a time. The agent was a bright young fellow, a bachelor, still under thirty.

He pondered for an instant the possibility of suggesting to Foster a visit after dinner to one of the local night spots. There was a new place of which he'd heard encouraging reports, dim lights and bright girls. But after a moment's reflection he dismissed the idea. Foster didn't strike him as the type to welcome the suggestion.

'Right, then,' he said. 'The lounge of the Falcon. A quarter to eight.'

At eight o'clock Alma Driscoll and her friend Rosie Trewin left Rosie's little terrace house and went along to the local pub for an hour or two while Rosie's husband obligingly kept an eye on the baby.

At half past ten Alma caught the last bus back to Abberley and made her way along the lane to Pinetrees. She looked in on the old couple, made them hot drinks, settled them down for the night and went off to bed, well pleased with her day.

Next morning she was awake early; she never slept late. By a quarter to seven she was washed and dressed, had tidied her bedroom and was on her way downstairs to make tea and take it up to the old folk.

She wasn't required to make breakfast or help them to wash and dress. A woman came in from the village at half past seven on alternate Friday mornings to see to all that and to keep an eye on things till the housekeeper returned on the mid-morning bus.

Alma carried the tray up to the main bedroom and knocked softly on the door. They were already awake, looking forward to a cup of tea.

Promptly at half past seven the village woman arrived and Alma was free to go back to Lynwood.

It was a fine morning, clear and mild, with a slight rustle of breeze. She met no one as she walked along the road, but the village was already stirring. She could hear the engine of a farm machine starting up, the lowing of cows, someone calling a dog across the fields.

She rounded a bend in the road and came in sight of Lynwood. The tall mass of the house was sharply outlined against the pearly blue sky. How well it looks standing up there, Alma thought, as she often did, admiring the elegant proportions, the lovely classic lines.

The lights were on in the front bedroom; no other lights showed in the house.

She quickened her pace. Mrs Foster was probably lying awake, restless after a poor night's sleep, finding time dragging till the door opened and someone carried in a welcome tray of tea.

Not much hope of the poor lady getting an early cup from Miss Jordan, Alma reflected; Miss Jordan was not the earliest of risers. It was usually eight o'clock before she showed her face downstairs, though always neat and trim when she did appear.

Alma reached the Pritchards' cottage, the nearest dwelling to Lynwood. Ned Pritchard was a retired farmworker, a widower, living with his son Bob who worked as a relief milker in the area. Ned still did a certain amount of work as a jobbing gardener and regularly put in a couple of days a week at Lynwood.

As Alma went past the cottage Bob Pritchard came out of an outhouse, carrying a bucket. He raised his hand and called out a greeting. She waved in reply and gave him a casual friendly word.

She went on up to the house and let herself in. Everything was quiet, no one stirring. She attended first to the cooker, glancing in at the oven to make sure the porridge was nicely done, but clicked her tongue in irritation when she found the porridge wasn't there.

Oh well, never mind, she thought after a moment. A nice pan of rolled oats wouldn't take long to cook on top of the stove, Mrs Foster wouldn't have to mind for once.

She set the pan on the stove, then put the kettle on to boil. She laid a tray and then at last took off her outdoor things. Mrs Foster's shampoo, she remembered, and put it on the tray beside the milk jug.

A few minutes later she carried the tray quietly up the back stairs. No sound from Miss Jordan's room—she must still be sound asleep.

As she approached Mrs Foster's bedroom she caught the sound of the radio, playing music. The poor lady had probably been lying awake goodness knew how long, with only the make-believe jollity of the disc jockey for company.

She knocked at the door. No reply. She knocked again, more loudly. Still no reply. She frowned, knocked again, even more loudly, without result.

She put her mouth against the door panel and said, 'Mrs Foster—it's me, Alma. I've brought you some tea.' Only the sound of the music came back to her, light and lilting. She tried the handle but the door was locked.

She set down the tray on a nearby table and went rapidly along the corridor into Mr Foster's room. She crossed to the connecting door and tried the handle but it resisted her.

She rapped forcefully on the panel, calling out loudly and recklessly, 'Mrs Foster! It's me, Alma! Are you all right?' Still no reply. The music ceased and a man's voice began to speak, crisp and cheerful.

She ran out of the room and along the corridor, down a few steps and round a corner, to Miss Jordan's room. There was no sound from within. She rapped loudly and without ceremony, calling out, 'Miss Jordan! Are you awake?'

There was a stir from inside and Miss Jordan's voice called back sleepily, 'Is that you, Alma?'

Without more ado Alma went in. The curtains were still drawn together. In the half-light Miss Jordan began to raise herself from the pillows.

'There's something wrong,' Alma said urgently. 'Mrs Foster—I can't make her hear. Her door's locked.'

Miss Jordan came fully awake. She flung back the clothes and sprang out of bed. She dragged on a dressing-gown, thrust her feet into slippers.

'I don't like it,' Alma said rapidly. 'I can hear the radio playing. I knocked and knocked but she doesn't answer.'

They left the room at a run. 'I tried to get in,' Alma said, 'but the doors are locked. Both doors.'

They reached Mrs Foster's room. Miss Jordan rattled the door handle, calling out, then she ran into Mr Foster's room, followed by Alma. She tried again.

'She tried to do something once before,' Alma said. 'Years ago. Before I came here. She took a lot of tablets.'

'Is there another key?' Miss Jordan said urgently. 'To either door?'

Alma frowned fiercely down at the floor. 'I can't think of one. I can't remember a spare key.'

'Then we'll have to get help. Someone to break the door down.'

'The Pritchards,' Alma said at once. 'Down at the cottage. You go, I'll stay here.' Miss Jordan, slimly built, would be able to run a good deal faster than Alma.

Alma stayed by the bedroom door, keeping up the fruitless calling and knocking. It seemed an age before she again heard the sound of running.

Young Bob Pritchard came racing into view along the corridor. 'Stand away!' he ordered as he reached the door.

He sprang back against the opposite wall, then leapt forward at the door, striking it with his raised foot. The door creaked. He went back to the wall and sprang again with all his strength. This time the panel gave.

As he struggled to get the door open Alma saw his father, Ned Pritchard, still quick and active at seventy, appear round the bend in the corridor, with Miss Jordan behind him. A smell of burning oatmeal floated up from the kitchen. The porridge, Alma registered—it's boiled over.

'You've managed it, then,' Ned called out as the door gave way. Alma followed Bob at a rush into the bedroom.

The lights were full on, the curtains drawn together. Beside the bed the radio played and sang.

Ned and Miss Jordan reached the door and came breathlessly in.

Mrs Foster was in a reclining position, leaning back against the lacy pillows. She wore a little jacket of peach-coloured satin over a nightdress of apricot chiffon. Her head had slipped to one side and her eyes were closed. Her face was peaceful, with a faint smile, as if she were sleeping. She looked young and pretty.

Her hands were relaxed on the lace coverlet. Under the fingers of one lay the silver-framed photograph of her father and under the fingers of the other a picture postcard.

Bob Pritchard leaned down and touched her forehead. With his other hand he circled her wrist. No pulse; she was icy cold. No one spoke. There was silence in the room except for the radio.

'Shall I phone the doctor?' Alma asked in a harsh breathless voice.

'You'd better.' Bob removed his hand from the wrist. 'But she's dead all right. Been dead for hours.'

He turned and switched off the radio. On the bedside table stood a tumbler holding a little water. Beside it a bottle of white tablets, two-thirds full.

Miss Jordan leaned across and felt the icy fingers. 'I'm afraid you're right.' She gave a long trembling sigh.

'She's done it again,' Ned Pritchard said from the foot of the bed.

They all turned to look at him. 'She tried once before,' he said. 'When her father died.'

He gazed sadly down at her. She looked no older now than she'd done then, nine years ago that was, must be. 'They found her in time then,' he said. 'They hushed it up. This time,' he added without surprise, 'she's managed to pull it off.'

CHAPTER 3

The inquest on Vera Foster was opened and adjourned a few days after her death, the body released for burial within a week. The funeral was small and private, as quiet as it was possible to make it in the circumstances.

The resumed inquest was set down for a date three weeks after the funeral.

Shortly before lunch on a Tuesday afternoon towards the end of October, Detective-Chief Inspector Kelsey stood at the window of his office in the central police station in Cannonbridge. He stared out at the pouring rain.

'The inquest on Mrs Foster this afternoon,' he said to Detective-Sergeant Lambert. 'You can drop me there, say a quarter to three.' He ran a hand over his springing hair, the colour of old carrots. 'I'll give you a ring when it's over. You can come along and pick me up.'

'It'll be suicide, of course,' Sergeant Lambert said. The inquiries into Mrs Foster's death had proceeded along a straightforward path. Perfectly clear-cut case.

The Chief nodded. No suggestion of anything else. According to the medical report Mrs Foster had swallowed a fatal dose of pain-killing tablets at a time when her husband was sitting with a highly respectable estate agent in full view of several people in the lounge of the Falcon Hotel seventy miles away in Lowesmoor. She was dead before her husband said goodnight to the agent and went upstairs to bed.

The Chief peered out at the driving rain with bleak hostility. 'Filthy day,' he said irritably. Rainy weather never agreed with him. Made him sneeze. Something to do with atmospheric pressure, he thought vaguely, made the lining of his nose congested.

'I detest October,' he added sourly. What he really detested was inquests. And, in particular, inquests on suicides. They always made him feel horribly depressed.

He felt a sudden powerful yearning for something sweet to thrust into his mouth. It was now some time since he'd succeeded in giving up smoking and it was only rarely that he still felt the old primitive longing for the death-dealing cigarette.

He'd managed very well on bags of toffees and bars of chocolate but now it seemed that even the confectionery substitute was forbidden.

'You've got to lose that,' the doctor had said at his last checkup, slapping the roll of flesh that strove against the Chief Inspector's waistband. 'If you've got to run after a villain you'll have a heart attack, like as not.'

'I don't run after villains any more,' Kelsey said. 'I let the lads chase about these days.'

'Can't rely on that,' the doctor said without sympathy. 'Never know your luck. You'll drop down dead one of these days, I shouldn't wonder.'

So now the soothing chocolate-covered peanuts were out, the cheering lumps of cracknel and nougat. Kelsey was reduced to biting through pencils and chewing the ends of ballpoint pens into distorted pulp.

His waistband had certainly slackened but his nerves had tautened. You can't win, he thought, staring out at the relentless rain. If the heart attacks don't get you, the ulcers will.

He turned abruptly from the window. 'Don't be late,' he told Sergeant Lambert with vague menace.

Always a gathering of cranks and ghouls at an inquest. If he was forced to stand about waiting for the car he'd be an easy prey for every local nutter eager to dredge up old grievances and many another new one invented on the spot. 'I phone you,' he said to Lambert, in case the message still hadn't got through, 'you come running.'

Promptly at a quarter to three Sergeant Lambert dropped the Chief outside the Cannonbridge courthouse. Kelsey made his way inside, saying what had to be said as briefly as possible to official or semi-official faces here and there.

He took his seat alone, making it clear by the expression on his craggy features and the set of his powerful shoulders that he wasn't seeking company.

A minute or two after he settled himself into his seat, Gerald Foster came into the courtroom. He looked pale and composed. But then he always looked pale and composed.

Kelsey watched him as he sat down. Until the recent enquiries he'd never spoken to Foster, although he knew who he was. In these unhappy dealings over the last few weeks he had found Foster direct and straightforward, easy to deal with.

Foster was considered locally to be a shrewd and soundly principled man of business. He was certainly respected in the community, although he lived quietly and took little part in local social activity.

Nor had the Chief Inspector ever met the late Mrs Foster, the subject of the inquest. As far as he could make out he had missed little. In the course of his enquiries the lady had come through to him as a right spoiled darling, a regular Daddy's little girl.

Kelsey had been acquainted with Daddy. A decent old chap, Duncan Murdoch, old-fashioned even in his own day; wing collars, striped trousers, silver-headed cane. Could hardly blame him for making such a close companion of Vera, his only child, particularly when you remembered that his wife had died at Vera's birth.

But Murdoch had certainly done his daughter no favour, he'd made her over-dependent on himself emotionally, made it difficult for her to form other relationships.

It had struck Kelsey in the course of his enquiries that Vera Foster seemed to have no close woman friend. Several women in the village of Abberley knew her, of course, but each in turn had said more or less, 'Of course, I didn't know her well, you couldn't really say I was a friend, more an acquaintance.' Certainly none of them seemed grief-stricken by her death, or even particularly moved or surprised by it.

The whole village, it appeared, had known of her earlier attempt to take her own life, when she had swallowed a large quantity of sleeping tablets prescribed for her father. There had been a strong attempt to hush it all up and the episode had certainly never reached Kelsey's ears. But it had got about the village all the same.

I doubt if Vera would have married at all if her father hadn't died, Kelsey ruminated. She was over thirty at the time of his death and had never, it seemed, had a boy-friend. She had gone about with her father—not that the pair of them went anywhere very much.

Easy to imagine how desperately she might have looked about after his sudden death for someone else to lean on—and there was no one but Gerald Foster.

She was lucky he was there, Kelsey reflected. In that unhappy time Foster was kind, helpful and sympathetic—according to the village. He wasn't some adventurer blown in on a wind of chance, capable of springing ugly surprises later, he was well known to Vera, liked, trusted and esteemed by her father.

He was experienced in the business, an employee of several years' standing, of proven worth, ready and able to take over the running, relieve her of worry.

And he was above all a single man, free to marry her.

If any part of that fortunate combination of circumstances had been different or absent, the Chief Inspector mused, Vera's life might have taken a very different course nine years ago.

The Lynwood housekeeper, Alma Driscoll, and the two Pritchard men, old Ned and his son Bob, followed Gerald Foster into the courtroom a few minutes later. Probably been given a lift by Foster, Kelsey thought. But they preserved a deferential distance between themselves and Foster when they took their seats; the three of them ranged themselves together at the end of a row.

Edith Jordan came in now. She had stayed on at Lynwood for some days after Vera Foster's death, to give what assistance she could. She had then been sent by the agency to another temporary post, that of assistant matron at Orchard House, a high-class boarding school for girls near Wychford, a small town ten miles to the west of Cannonbridge.

Kelsey's eyes rested on Miss Jordan. She had a certain air of breeding, of natural elegance. She was dressed in a dark grey tailored suit with a white blouse and a small hat; she wore no make-up. Her whole appearance suggested native taste and refinement. She looked the kind who could be relied on to keep her head in an emergency. Certainly Doctor Tredgold thought highly of her.

Not what you would call attractive, Kelsey pondered, and yet her features and general aspect had nothing irregular or ill-proportioned about them.

I think it's mainly because she gives the impression of having no interest in men, Kelsey concluded after a few moments' thought. The absence of those vibrations makes a man think she's not attractive—a woman might see her differently, he reflected.

He looked along the row to where Alma Driscoll sat glancing about with lively interest. Alma was shorter than Edith Jordan, plumper, with a far less lithe and supple figure. She had no real advantage in looks that you could put your finger on. True, she had a fine head of auburn hair, but then Miss Jordan had a good head of dark hair.

But any man would call Alma Driscoll attractive— probably, the Chief considered, because Alma found men attractive, was interested in them, didn't disguise that interest.

Miss Jordan inclined her head politely towards Mr Foster, then she took her seat beside Alma Driscoll. She leaned forward and exchanged a word and a pleasant smile with the two Pritchard men, then she and Alma began to chat in hushed tones.

Foster remained staring ahead. It must be an ordeal for him, Kelsey thought, waiting for proceedings to begin, having to go through it all yet again, hearing the same painful story once more from successive lips.

Doctor Tredgold came hurrying up the courtroom steps only a couple of minutes before the town-hall clock struck three. He glanced over at Kelsey as he came in and gave him a friendly nod, then he sat down at a little distance from the Lynwood party.

Kelsey saw that the doctor's face wore a look of slight unease. No mystery about the cause of that unease. Tredgold couldn't be happy about the fact that he'd prescribed another bottle of pain-killing tablets for Mrs Foster, tablets which she made use of almost at once to take her own life, when he knew that she had once before attempted suicide.

True, that earlier attempt had been passed off at the time by all concerned as an accidental overdose, but Tredgold knew well enough what that meant.

Not that the Chief Inspector was disposed to be critical of the doctor. He'd come across him many times over the years. He liked and respected him, had always found him helpful, a man of integrity and sound professional ability.

Easy enough to say with hindsight that the character of the dead woman was known to Tredgold, that he could have prescribed the tablets in much smaller quantities or entrusted their care and use entirely to Miss Jordan.

But there had been only the one previous attempt at suicide and that was nine years ago at a time of sudden and highly unusual stress. And a doctor didn't perform his work in some ideal society but in the real world where haste and overwork, forgetfulness and irritation, hunger and fatigue all played their part.

I certainly wouldn't like to be held up to public censure for every error I've made over the years, Kelsey thought with a shudder.

The clock struck the hour. At all events Tredgold's lucky with the coroner, Kelsey thought as the proceedings began.

The coroner was a retired doctor who knew Tredgold well, belonged to the same golf club. Not likely to strive for press headlines by making noble utterances about the duties and responsibilities of the medical profession.

The afternoon wore on with no surprises. There were sympathetic looks for Gerald Foster as he gave his evidence. He stood looking straight ahead, his hands hanging loosely at his sides, his slight figure held stiffly upright.

Yes, he had known of his wife's earlier attempt to take her own life. He had been one of the two people who had found her on that occasion, it was he who broke down the bedroom door and summoned the doctor. That was before he and Vera were married, when he had been an employee of her late father.

Yes, the marriage had been happy, he would call it very happy. He and his wife were well suited, there were no worries, financial or otherwise.

No, it had not seemed foolish to leave the tablets within reach of his wife. She had been subject to attacks of sciatica for some years, had had access to pain-killing tablets during all that time, with no untoward occurrence. And the earlier overdose was nine years before, in most exceptional circumstances. He had never had reason to suppose there would be any repetition.

He had phoned his wife as he always did when he was away, he rang her just after nine in the evening, from the Falcon Hotel in Lowesmoor. She had sounded very much as usual, she said nothing to cause him alarm.

No, she had left no letter — nor had she left any letter in the previous attempt. The card which lay under her fingers was one she had always treasured; it was the last written communication she had received from her father, a postcard he had sent her shortly before his death, on one of his rare absences from Lynwood.

The card was normally kept in a drawer of a small desk in her bedroom. The last words of the message had been heavily underlined. No, they had not been underlined by Duncan Murdoch when he wrote the card, nor had they been underlined the last time Foster had seen the card, which he thought must have been three or four months ago.

His wife would sometimes take the card out and read it, would talk to him about her father, and so on. Yes, he would definitely have remembered if the words had been underlined, he would have noticed it, would have commented on the fact to his wife.

He had no doubt that it was his wife who had underlined the words just before she took the fatal overdose.

The pen she must have used lay on the bedside table. The sentence she had underlined read: See you very soon, my dearest.

There was a hush in the courtroom as Foster spoke the words. He stood for some moments with his head bowed.

Could he in any way account for his wife's action in taking the fatal dose? the coroner asked gently.

'I can only suppose,' Foster answered in a tone of profound regret, 'that the sciatica was more depressing than I realized. And the tablets must also have been more lowering than I realized. My wife was a woman of impulse. And she didn't like —' he hesitated — 'she didn't like the fact that she was no longer a young girl.' He closed his eyes briefly. 'She found it difficult to accept.'

Yes, he was some years younger than his wife. Not that this had made or ever would have made any difference to his feeling for her. But yes, it could have heightened her own sense of the passing of her youth, she certainly never liked to think of his being younger than herself, she would refer to it sometimes when she was in low spirits. Yes, he would agree that she could be fairly described as an emotional woman.

No, there was no spare key to either of the two doors leading into his wife's bedroom. Or at least not to his knowledge.

Miss Jordan took the stand next. She gave her evidence in a calm and precise manner.

No, she had known nothing of the earlier attempt at suicide by Mrs Foster. She had been engaged some two weeks before Mrs Foster's death to assist the lady during her illness. She had no previous acquaintance with Mrs Foster or with anyone else in the household, she had never in fact set foot in Abberley before going to Lynwood.

She had given Mrs Foster one of the tablets with a beaker of drinking chocolate — Mrs Foster's usual night-time beverage — at a quarter to ten, and then settled her down for the night. She returned the bottle of tablets to the shelf in the little wall cabinet over the wash-basin in the bedroom. This was where such bottles were normally kept.

Yes, in her opinion Mrs Foster was perfectly capable of getting out of bed and walking across to the cabinet and then to the desk. She had thought Mrs Foster a good deal better than she would admit.

She had formed the impression that Mrs Foster was a lady who liked a little extra attention, didn't object to staying in bed, was perhaps inclined to remain there longer than was necessary. She had said as much to Doctor Tredgold on his last visit; he had not disagreed with her.

Yes, looking back now, she would agree that perhaps this attitude of Mrs Foster's could have been an indication of depression. And yes, she would agree now with Mr Foster's opinion that the sciatica could have been a good deal more lowering than any of them had realized.

Mrs Foster had asked for the photograph of her father earlier in the day, had indeed fallen asleep in the course of her morning nap holding the photograph. Miss Jordan had later returned it to its usual place on top of the dressing-chest.

No, Mrs Foster had not again asked her for the photograph during the evening. She must have got out of bed and fetched it after Miss Jordan had left her for the night.

Miss Jordan had never seen the postcard before, nor did she know of its existence. Mrs Foster had never shown it to her or mentioned it.

She had heard no sound in the night, had not been disturbed. She had been tired, had gone to bed as soon as she had settled Mrs Foster. She had fallen asleep at once, had slept soundly till wakened next morning by Mrs Driscoll knocking on her bedroom door.

No, she had seen and observed nothing amiss in the

domestic atmosphere at Lynwood. She had thought the marriage happy and Mr Foster an attentive and affectionate husband.

Ned Pritchard, smart in his best navy-blue suit and pale blue shirt, wasn't called to give evidence — to his deep disappointment. His son Bob was duly called and in the eyes of his proud father did well, spoke up clearly, told what he knew, didn't stumble or rattle on.

Yes, all the lights were on when he broke down the door of Mrs Foster's bedroom. Both doors to the room were locked; both keys had been removed from the locks and lay on top of the dressing-chest in Mrs Foster's bedroom.

No, he saw no letter, though of course he didn't go searching round the room. Just the postcard and the photograph, as if Mrs Foster had been holding one in each hand at the last.

When Doctor Tredgold took the stand he looked old and tired. He had been called out at four in the morning to a patient in the next village who was suffering from a violent gall-bladder attack.

When the doctor returned home he didn't go back to bed, knowing from experience that he wouldn't be able to sleep again. He had stayed up, dealing with paperwork until the start of his normal working day. He felt now in an exhausted, dreamlike state. While waiting to be called he had difficulty in keeping his eyes open.

The old boy really ought to retire, the reporter from the local paper thought without-sympathy, himself a bright lad of twenty-five, still under the illusion that his own vigorous youth was under some kind of exceptional protection and would last for ever.

The coroner, looking at his old friend, listening to his account, remembered a time or two during his own years in general practice when he had taken the stand to give evidence in not very dissimilar cases.

And a time or two when he had been lucky not to have

been called. And a great many times when he had felt at three o'clock in the afternoon after a long and semi-sleepless night and difficult morning, very much as Doctor Tredgold looked now.

The doctor gave his evidence in a flat clear tone. Yes, he knew that Mrs Foster—at that time of course still Miss Vera Murdoch—had suffered an overdose of sleeping tablets on the day of her father's funeral. He had been summoned to treat her.

No, it had never been represented to him as an attempt at suicide. It had been described, both by the lady herself and those connected with her, as an accidental overdose arising from fatigue, strain, grief, and so on. No, he had had no difficulty in accepting this account of what had happened.

It was several years ago and the circumstances of Mrs Foster's life had very much changed since then. He had felt she was living a normal life with every chance of stability and well-being. He believed she was happily married and had an excellent husband.

Yes, he had from time to time treated her for nervous upsets, bouts of insomnia and the like, but these minor distresses were in his experience very common among ladies, particularly childless ladies no longer in their first youth.

No, he certainly hadn't looked on her as a potential suicide risk when he prescribed for her sciatica. No, it hadn't occurred to him to ask Miss Jordan to take charge of all medicines.

Even if it had occurred to him he wouldn't have considered it a very practical proposition. After Miss Jordan left—what then? Was he to see that every pill and tablet in the house was locked up, that only Mr Foster or Miss Driscoll had the key?

No reasonable medical colleague could quarrel with that attitude, the coroner reflected as the doctor left the stand. He well knew the fusses, wheedlings, complaints, of which these verge-of-middle-age females were capable; no family doctor could stand up to them for long.

And if Tredgold had withheld the tablets — the shops were full of aspirins and half a dozen other pills and concoctions that could be lethal if taken in a large enough dose. There were such things as razor-blades, knives, guns, high windows and road traffic. Over the years the coroner had encountered all the ways in which determined persons can end their own existence.

Alma Driscoll gave evidence next. A niece of old Matt Bateman, Chief Inspector Kelsey had discovered. Bateman was, as it were, known to the local force. There had been a police constable stationed in Abberley village until a few years ago and in those days Matt's rural activities resulted from time to time in little chats between the constable and Matt. But Matt had never actually appeared in court on any charge.

Alma had taken great pains with her appearance for this public occasion. After a good deal of thought she had regretfully decided that it was only fitting she should wear a hat.

But in order not to obscure the full glory of her auburn hair, freshly washed and set, gleaming under the court-room lights — for the afternoon continued dull and rainy — she had put on her smallest piece of headgear. This was her wedding and christening hat, no more than a few ribbons and flowers with a bloom of veiling. It gave her appearance a light-hearted holiday air.

The coroner questioned her in some detail about Mrs Foster's state of mind, in particular during the weeks immediately before her death.

Well, yes, Alma had to admit, Mrs Foster was more moody than usual during that time, more given to sudden fits of ill-temper.

Yes, the sciatica did seem to pull her down, but then it

always did; Alma had got used to this, expected it, wasn't upset by it, paid it little attention.

And she had got used to Mrs Foster's outbursts and tricky temperament. Mrs Foster was a highly-strung lady, Alma knew how to manage her well enough, didn't let it bother her overmuch. It was all a matter of knowing how to handle people. She had a good situation at Lynwood, took such things in her stride, counted herself lucky to have such a good home.

But yes, looking back, she would agree that it was very likely that Mrs Foster had been rather more depressed than Alma had realized.

She hesitated, then braced her shoulders and glanced up at the coroner with an air of being about to say something she felt must be said.

'The way I look at it now, and with all due respect to all concerned—' She pulled a handkerchief from the pocket of her coat and began to twist it between her fingers. 'I think we'd all got into the habit of treating the poor lady as if she was exaggerating—me as well as everybody else.' She gave a quick dab at her eyes. 'As if she was making half of it up.'

She began to make a little crying sound, but talked on through it. 'We all behaved as if she wasn't really in all that much pain, we never took it seriously.' She began to cry in earnest.

The coroner leaned forward, told her not to distress herself, asked if she would like a glass of water but she shook her head. 'Just because she was a bit spoiled,' she said in a little rush. 'I'm sure now she suffered a lot more than any of us thought.'

She drew a long sighing breath and stood up very straight. She gave her eyes a final dab and put her handkerchief back in her pocket with an air of resolution. She put up a hand and touched her hair, her gossamer trifle of a hat.

The Chief Inspector looked across the courtroom as she left the stand a few minutes later amid a little murmur of sympathy. Foster was leaning forward in his seat, his head lowered, his chin supported on one hand, the elbow resting on his knee. His face was obscured from Kelsey's vision.

There was a little shifting and movement in the public benches, a surreptitious glancing at watches when the coroner began to glance through his notes a little later.

He pursed his lips as he turned a page. It all looked perfectly straightforward. Mrs Foster had clearly decided to take her own life, for reasons which appeared to stem entirely from her own personality. The police had been able to uncover no suggestion or anything else, no financial or other difficulties, no romantic attachment outside the marriage on the part of either the dead woman or her husband.

Mrs Foster had behaved as she might be expected to behave in the light of that decision. She had chosen a night when her husband was away, the housekeeper out, and the only other person sleeping in the house a woman who knew nothing of her patient's history, who was a stranger to Lynwood and Abberley, unacquainted with local gossip.

Just as well there were no children of the marriage, the coroner reflected, these cases were always a good deal more distressing when a young family was left without a mother.

Vera Foster struck him as a typical neurotic, demanding and self-centred, unable to accept the hard facts of the passing of the years. A woman who, like the rest of her kind, failed to develop her own resources, looked to the poor husband to supply the gaps left by her own deficiencies, was loud in complaint at any fancied neglect.

Even the decision — or more properly, in all likelihood, the impulse — to take her own life, the coroner saw as the huge central accusation designed to remain imprinted for ever in the brain of the spouse, disseminating and perpetuating feelings of guilt, poisoning the rest of the unfortunate man's life with remorse and anguished memories.

He shuffled his notes together. A rotten job, sitting as coroner. Depressing, if one allowed it to be. If it wasn't for his strong sense of public duty he'd give it up tomorrow. But someone had to do it and it cheered him sometimes to think he might at least do it better than the next man.

He felt an unexpected surge of sympathy for poor Vera Foster. He had known the taste of depression himself, had looked more than once into the dark pit that opens in the night, in the silent hours, the lonely time.

He flicked a single reassuring look at Tredgold, just to let him know nothing too bad was coming his way, then he cleared his throat and began to speak.

Well, that's that, Chief Inspector Kelsey said to himself with relief when it was all over and the courtroom was clearing. The coroner had left the court, it was the last inquest of the day.

Kelsey felt a sudden acute pang of hunger. It isn't true hunger, the doctor had told him unsympathetically. It's just a need for comfort, something to put in your mouth, a hangover from babyhood. Try nibbling raw carrots or a stick of celery.

I'd look well with the colour of my hair, sitting in public places chomping on carrots, Kelsey thought sourly.

He hunched himself into his seat, waiting for the room to empty. Apples, he thought with a flash of inspiration, that might be the answer. He wouldn't look such an almighty fool if he took an apple from his pocket and bit into it. It might even lend a certain rustic charm to his appearance. Homely, disarming.

Then he sighed. He wasn't all that fond of apples, they gave him indigestion. About two a year was his idea of enough apples.

Ah — what about nuts? He could scarcely refrain from smiling at the brilliance of the notion. Nuts and raisins. Potato crisps. He liked all those.

He began to feel almost cheerful at the prospect of the many agreeable nibbles opening up before him, but then gloom descended abruptly again. Those luscious goodies were no whit less fattening than sweets and chocolates, no more likely to receive the blessing of his doctor.

Chewing-gum? he pondered with the last rays of hope, but he was already beginning to shake his head even as the idea struck him. He had a swift vision of the Superintendent, a gentleman who would undoubtedly hold decided views on gum-chewing Chief Inspectors. He gave a long low sigh, leaned back and closed his eyes.

When the press of folk had died down Kelsey got to his feet and went off to phone Sergeant Lambert at the station. There was a room along the corridor where he knew there was a phone. He made his call and then stood by the window, staring idly out at the afternoon.

The room was stuffy and after a moment he opened the transom light. Noises drifted up from the street. The sky was even darker now, the rain had ceased but it looked as if it would start again at any moment with renewed force.

He heard the sound of voices almost below him and he glanced down into the street. A few feet away, over to his right, he could see the Lynwood party getting into Foster's car. Alma Driscoll took the passenger seat and the Pritchard men, father and son, settled themselves into the back.

Near the car bonnet Miss Jordan stood talking to Foster. Kelsey could hear the general drift of their conversation, which was polite and formal.

Foster was offering Miss Jordan a lift back to the boarding school at Wychford. She thanked him, said she needn't trouble him, she was going on the bus, it was very convenient. After another minute or two they shook hands.

Miss Jordan bent down and spoke to the passengers in the car, then she walked away. Foster closed the rear door, stooping to speak to Ned Pritchard. As he straightened up he turned his head and looked away, over to his left.

Kelsey followed his glance and saw Edith Jordan pause for a moment and glance back at Foster. Foster was shielded from casual eyes — but not from the glance of the Chief Inspector looking down from above.

Foster gave Miss Jordan a single sharp little nod. At the same time he raised his right hand in a small clear gesture, the thumb and middle finger touching, describing a circle, a small controlled jerk of movement, the gesture of success, triumph. He smiled at Miss Jordan as he did so. His eyes were half-closed; it was an intimate smile, a little pout of the lips, full of satisfaction, a secret shared.

Kelsey flashed a look at Edith Jordan. She was half-smiling back at Foster. She gave one tiny nod, then the smiling look vanished and was replaced by her customary air of calm and dignified composure.

She turned and began to make her way along the street, towards the bus stop.

Kelsey felt the hairs prickle along the back of his neck. He remained where he was, motionless, his gaze fixed on the vehicle below.

Foster got into the driving seat, said something to his passengers and set the car in motion.

The Chief Inspector was still standing in the same position when Sergeant Lambert appeared in the doorway of the room a few minutes later.

'There you are, Chief!' Lambert said. 'I couldn't make

out where you'd got to.'

Kelsey made no reply, didn't so much as glance round. Lambert came further into the room. 'I've brought the car,' he said. 'Are you ready to go?' Still the Chief said nothing.

Lambert came right up to him. 'Is anything wrong?' he asked. The Chief turned his head and gave him a blind stare. 'The inquest,' Lambert said. 'Everything go all right? No surprises? Suicide verdict?'

The Chief gave a single nod. Then he made a sudden turn from the window. 'But it wasn't suicide,' he said with fierce energy. 'I'll take my dying oath on that. They pulled it off between them. Foster and Edith Jordan. It was murder.'

CHAPTER 4

Lambert stared back at the Chief.

'I saw them.' Kelsey gestured at the window. 'Down there. A few minutes ago. They exchanged a look.'

'Is that all?' Lambert said in astonishment.

'It's enough.'

'One single look?'

'Foster said goodbye to her. Everything as you'd expect. The others were there in the car, looking on, Mrs Driscoll and the Pritchards.' Kelsey described what he'd seen, the look, the gesture, the exchange of smiles. 'I'm as certain now it was murder as if I'd seen them do it.' He struck a fist into his palm. 'They'll not get away with it! I'll make sure they don't!'

Lambert mentioned the Chief's next appointment. 'You'll be late if we don't leave now,' he warned.

Kelsey fell into line beside him and began to walk with him to the door. 'You don't say anything!' he said with force. 'I presume you have some opinion?'

'It doesn't seem much to go on,' Lambert said diplomatically. He well knew the Chief's aversion to inquests, the tricks that aversion was likely to play on his spirit and imagination.

'You didn't see the look,' Kelsey said in a voice of challenge.

'Surely the verdict means the case is closed,' Lambert said. 'Whatever you may suspect now, we can hardly go round trying to open it up again.' They'd look well walking into Lynwood with open notebooks, starting a whole new enquiry into the circumstances of Mrs Foster's death. Foster couldn't be expected to tolerate it. And Lambert wouldn't blame him.

Kelsey chewed the inside of his cheek with fierce concentration. He went out of the courthouse and down the steps in silent absorption, leaving Lambert to nod and murmur at any official faces they encountered.

As they reached the car Kelsey said, 'I'll leave it for the moment.' He didn't have much option if he was going to give any attention to his next appointment. 'I'll sleep on it, see what I think about it in the morning.'

Over the years he'd perfected a trick that worked well enough. Just before he went to sleep he directed a stream of intense thought at the matter to be decided. He left a powerful command with his subconscious, placing the matter in the hands of that agent, directing it to consider and reach a conclusion by morning.

Then he laid his head on the pillow, dismissed the matter from his conscious thoughts and went to sleep with cheerful confidence.

The method didn't always work, and the conclusions reached by this invisible subordinate didn't always justify the method, but the Chief still retained confidence in it. And he didn't know any better method. Certainly, lying awake half the night trying to puzzle something out had nothing to recommend it. He used to try that a long time ago; all it did was blunt his brain, weary his eyelids, cloud his thoughts and inflame his temper next day.

When Kelsey strode into the central police station next morning he encountered Sergeant Lambert in the reception hall. Lambert was standing by the desk, blowing his nose, frowning down at his feet, trying to decide which of half a dozen objectionable tasks he ought to force himself to tackle first.

Kelsey marched up to him and stuck a forefinger in his back. Lambert glanced round. One look at Kelsey's light green eyes, glittering with the energetic mischievous look the sergeant knew well, told him that vigorous doings were afoot.

Vigorous doings for Sergeant Lambert, that is. The Chief had reached the stage in his career when he preferred vigorous doings to be carried out by other parties, with himself directing, and occasionally — very occasionally — cheering on the sidelines.

Lambert couldn't immediately recall what it was that had lit the glitter in the Chief's eyes.

'Come on!' Kelsey said, jerking his great carroty head in the direction of his office. 'I want to talk to you.' Lambert followed obediently in the Chief's wake.

Kelsey stopped every couple of yards to direct questions, comments and miscellaneous observations at various constables and sergeants who crossed their path.

At last they reached his office. He flung open the door. 'I've made up my mind!' he announced as soon as they were over the threshold. 'The Foster case,' he added, seeing Lambert's face still closed and uncomprehending.

Lambert closed his eyes briefly. He'd forgotten the Chief's moment of vision by the courthouse window. 'It's no good standing there blinking like a mule,' Kelsey said with vigour.

He flopped into his chair and jerked a finger at Lambert, instructing him to sit down. Lambert obeyed.

'I knew the moment I opened my eyes this morning,' the Chief said with satisfaction. 'I could see the two of them standing there, looking at each other. That look's burned into my brain. It was no ordinary conventional look. It was the glance of conspirators.'

He sat up. 'I'm not a jackass!' he said challengingly to Lambert, who had said nothing, offered no gesture or movement to encourage the Chief in his lunacy.

'I can read a look as well as the next man!' The Chief smashed a great fist down on the desk, causing half his morning mail to leap up in the air and the other half to descend to the floor in a dishevelled pile. 'I say it was murder! They were in it together! Planned it and carried it out between them!'

Lambert got to his feet and began to scrabble about on the floor, collecting the envelopes. Kelsey glared down at him. 'Don't tell me I'm an idiot!' He struck his hands together. 'What that glance said was: We pulled it off! We fooled them!'

The Chief jumped to his feet and began to stride about the room. 'Consider the time and place: The pair of them have just left a courtroom after a suicide verdict on the woman who was the wife of one of them and the patient of the other. What legitimate reason could that man have for levelling that glance at that woman in those circumstances?' He dropped back into his chair.

Lambert stood up and placed the letters on the desk. As he did so he let out a long loud deliberate sigh. Kelsey tilted back his chair and regarded him with a level look totally devoid of theatrical content, cold and assessing.

'I don't say you're wrong,' Lambert said in answer to that shrewd glance. 'But I do say it's impossible to open the case again.'

'We could just have a little poke round.' The Chief

waved a hand. 'Wouldn't do any harm.'

'It could do a great deal of harm.' As the Chief well knew. They couldn't go asking a fresh string of questions at Lynwood. Or pursue Edith Jordan over to Orchard House School. Not without giving rise to conjecture. And once that kind of whisper started there was no way on earth it could be stopped again. Two lives could be permanently ruined.

'What if you're totally wrong?' Lambert said. 'If they're both completely innocent?'

Kelsey gave a noisy sigh that was almost a groan. 'Do you think I haven't thought about that?' He banged his fist on the desk. 'I still say they did it.' He made a jerking movement of his head. 'I've made up my mind. We'll have another look into it.' He smote the desk again but more lightly, and with half an eye to the letters. 'This time we're going to nail them.'

Lambert went back to his chair and sat down with an air of deliberation. 'Right, then,' he said, always a man to recognize the inescapable. And the fact that a sergeant is only a sergeant — and that none of the half-dozen chores awaiting him were any more appealing than this one.

Kelsey put the tips of his fingers together. 'Some of the facts we previously accepted,' he said with a judicial air, 'now appear capable of more than one interpretation. It looked so obviously suicide, we interpreted everything in the light of suicide.'

He picked up a pen and began to stab it into a memo pad. 'What I propose to do now is look at it all again, interpret it all afresh, this time in the light of murder. See if in that light all the known facts can be made to jell.'

He frowned and continued stabbing. 'That exchange of glances. That strikes me as quite contrary to the relationship we were given to believe exists between Foster and Edith Jordan. It suggests there is a public face to their relationship and another more private face of which we know nothing. It suggests they have known each other longer and more intimately than they admit to. I find it difficult to imagine any innocent reason for this discrepancy.'

He threw the pen down on the desk and got to his feet. He crossed to the window and stood staring up at the windy sky. Then he went back to his desk. He opened a file, riffled through the pages.

'Edith Jordan was sent to Lynwood by the Cannonbridge Staff Agency,' Sergeant Lambert said. 'It's a highly respectable concern. Surely they would have checked her references when they first took her on. And Doctor Tredgold spoke very highly of her.'

'We don't know how long she's worked for the agency,' Kelsey said. 'Who she is. Where she came from. What kind of background.' They hadn't bothered to find out, it hadn't seemed necessary.

He looked up at Lambert. 'We don't even know she came from the agency at all. She told us she did. Foster told us she did. But we never checked. She could have come from the moon for all we actually know.' He set his jaw. 'All that will have to be gone into now.'

He sat in silence for a moment. 'Motive,' he said with a massive frown. No point in attempting to pursue any of this unless he could come up with some credible motive, powerful enough to drive a man to plot the murder of his wife.

For if indeed it was murder, then it was no unpremeditated act committed on the impulse of sudden furious emotion, but a cold-blooded murder, well thought out and carefully executed.

'There's got to be a pretty powerful motive for Edith Jordan as well,' Kelsey said. Possibly a totally different motive from Foster's, but one that meshed in with his. 'Love or money.' Usually one or the other. Or a mixture of both.

'Are you suggesting some kind of love affair between Foster and Edith Jordan?' Lambert asked. She struck him as a confirmed spinster. But maybe she was an accomplished actress, able to project what image she wished. She was certainly an able and intelligent woman.

'It's conceivable,' Kelsey said. 'Just about.' Miss Jordan was ten years older than Foster, but then Foster was accustomed to an older woman, maybe that was where his taste lay. Kelsey moved his shoulders. His own tastes were otherwise.

'It could be of course,' he said, 'that Foster is involved with a woman, some woman other than Edith Jordan.' Though they hadn't heard a whisper of anything like that during their enquiries.

'Suppose that is the case,' Kelsey went on. 'Suppose he wanted to get rid of his wife, marry this other woman, simply decided to hire Edith Jordan to help him. In due course when it's all over, all talk has died down, Foster can go ahead and marry his lady love.

'No suspicion attaches to this lady, she's in no way involved in Vera's death, she probably knows nothing about it, accepts it as suicide. She may never have set foot in Lynwood, may not be known to a soul in Abberley village, may never have clapped eyes on Vera.'

He struck the desk. 'And Edith Jordan, having done her job and been paid her fee, isn't seen again in Abberley. Neat little plan.'

'Straightforward hire and reward?' Lambert said.

'That's it. If Vera is to be murdered, then Foster certainly can't do it himself. No shred of suspicion must attach to him. He must be out of the house at the time, preferably at some considerable distance. He must be visibly otherwise engaged, in circumstances which will put him completely above suspicion, which will admit of no possible dispute later.'

He sat back in his chair. 'As, for instance, having dinner with a highly respectable business associate in the Falcon Hotel seventy miles away in Lowesmoor. And sitting talking to that same associate in the public lounge until bedtime, until in fact well after Vera is dead.'

He massaged his jaw. 'So if Foster can't do the deed himself, someone else must. Someone no one would suspect of any crime, someone previously unknown to the victim, no connection of any kind with her, no apparent motive.' He pursed his lips. 'Someone exactly like Edith Jordan.'

'Paying over a substantial sum of money to Edith Jordan,' Lambert said. 'Wouldn't that be a risky business? If suspicion should arise later on?'

'Plenty of ways of paying her without passing a cheque through either of their accounts,' Kelsey said briskly. 'Foster walks into a jeweller's, some place he's not known, he buys a valuable piece of jewellery, gives it to Miss Jordan. Later on she sells it in London. Who's to connect the purchase and the sale?'

'You're saying, of course,' Lambert said, 'that Foster must have known Edith Jordan before the agency sent her to nurse his wife.'

'Of course I'm saying that,' Kelsey said impatiently. 'My whole theory rests on the assumption that they must have known each other for longer than they admit. It's hardly likely Edith Jordan walked into Lynwood as a total stranger and Foster went up to her and said: If you help me to dispose of my wife I'll buy you a diamond necklace.'

He rapped the desk. 'You'll have to get cracking on all this. Find out if Foster's marriage was on the rocks. Or heading that way. If there was ever any talk of divorce, not just recently, but at any time in the marriage.'

Foster could have raised the matter of divorce way back and found it stridently opposed by Vera. He might then have decided to make an appearance of abandoning the idea, patched things up with Vera, while at the same time

forming a resolve to pursue less conventional ways of
ending his marriage.

'Find out if Foster had been straying,' Kelsey said. 'If he
had ever strayed at any time in the marriage, if he was the
type to stray.'

'If he does have some other female,' Lambert said,
'he'll surely be cooling it at present.' He'd probably have
been cooling it for some time before the murder. Wisdom
would dictate he should start to cool it as soon as he
seriously contemplated making an end to Vera.

'We may have to go back quite some time to uncover
anything,' Kelsey said. 'Alma Driscoll's been — what —
eight years at Lynwood. She might know something.'

'I suppose there's no question of Alma being the lady?'

Kelsey pulled down the corners of his mouth. Difficult
to imagine Foster falling for Alma's cheerful, flashy looks.
'Can't see it,' he said. But he'd keep an open mind.

'Foster doesn't go away all that often,' Lambert pointed
out. Hardly often enough to be able to sustain an under-
cover liaison at any substantial distance from Lynwood.
'If there is someone — someone other than Edith Jordan or
Alma Driscoll — then I imagine she'd have to be fairly
local.'

'Possibly.' Kelsey twisted a pen in his fingers. 'Then
there's the other alternative. Money. Find out if Foster
benefits financially by his wife's death. In any way at all,
not just the obvious ways. We didn't go into that in any
detail.'

But one thing they had checked — Foster carried no
insurance on Vera's life, not one single penny.

Kelsey threw the pen in the air and caught it again.
'Foster's solicitors, Lawson and Dulcott —'

'I'll have a word there,' Lambert put in. He had some
acquaintance with a clerk in Lawson and Dulcott, a
young man he'd come across in court work, had been able
to do a favour for more than once.

'I'll look in at the bank,' Kelsey said. Foster banked at the Central and the manager there had been at school with Kelsey. They'd copied each other's homework, smoked cigarettes together behind the gym, fought over the same girls. 'No problems there,' he said with massive and well-placed confidence in those powerful primitive bonds.

'Was Foster born here in Cannonbridge?' Lambert asked. The sergeant was a comparative newcomer to this side of the county; he gathered that Foster was more or less a local man but he knew nothing more precise about his origins.

Kelsey pondered. 'I can't say for sure. He's from somewhere round these parts but I don't know the family. Should be easy enough to find out.'

He stood up. 'All this is strictly *sub rosa*. To be fitted in with your normal duties.' He jabbed a finger at the air. 'Bear in mind your middle name is discretion. And your surname. And that name which was given to you by your godparents in baptism.' He grinned. 'And any secret names so terrible they're spoken only by devils in the dark of the moon.'

CHAPTER 5

The Chief Inspector discovered later in the morning that the demands of his day carried his feet past the classic portals of the Central Bank in Market Street. It would be foolish not to take the opportunity to slip inside and have a word with old Greasy Grenville.

According to the delectable young lady at the counter, Old Greasy — but she referred to him as Mr Grenville — was in his office. She passed a message back through a subordinate and chatted amiably to the Chief as he waited.

In theory the Chief subscribed to fashionable ideas of female equality—as many another wise man found it expedient to do—but he was just old enough not to have swallowed the ideas along with his mother's milk, and so had never fully been able to accept them as part of the natural structure of life.

He couldn't, for instance, totally rid himself of the notion that banks decorated their front counters with beautiful young women employed solely for that purpose, and that all the real eyeball-reddening toil was done by pimply rat-faced males behind screens of thoughtfully obscure glass.

When Kelsey was admitted to Old Greasy's office a few minutes later, Old Greasy sprang at once to his feet. He was actually a handsome and well set up man, well groomed and well turned out. He smiled broadly as Kelsey entered, he came round the desk and struck the Chief a crippling blow on the arm.

'Copperknob!' he said with old and deep affection. In comradely reply Kelsey dealt him a sharp crack on the shoulder with his surviving fist.

Ten minutes later Kelsey came out of Grenville's sanctum, smiled at a second beauty queen who had taken up her station at the counter, and went out into Market Street.

According to Grenville there were no money troubles of any kind in the Cannonbridge Thrift Society. 'If all our customers were like Gerald Foster,' he said, 'banking would be a piece of cake.'

He considered Vera Foster to have been of a cautious, even timid, business disposition, but he rated Foster as a man of sound judgment, well able to estimate a market, assess a risk, size up the creditworthiness of assorted citizens.

'Back in the spring, to give you just one example,' Grenville said, 'Foster bought a small run-down plating works over at Lineholt.' Lineholt was a town some twenty miles from Cannonbridge. 'He bought it cheap and he immediately set about gingering it up. He went into the whole thing very thoroughly, took enormous trouble to find the right man to put in as manager. The business is already beginning to show a profit.'

In none of Foster's business endeavours was there any problem with cash flow, no nerve-racking balancing on a knife-edge every month or quarter-day.

Furthermore — and here Grenville smiled in approbation — Foster had no deep and fundamental vanity, that curse of the rising businessman. He had no wish to transfer the business to larger and more showy premises, no urge to go in for expensive entertaining, to drive round town in a glittering petrol-swilling monster in order to impress the competition.

Grenville had seen more up-and-coming entrepreneurs bite the dust because of vanity — their own or their wives' — than from any other single cause, except shortage of capital. 'And Foster certainly has no lack of capital,' Grenville added.

'He had an account here with us before he married Vera Murdoch,' he told Kelsey. 'He opened the account with his first week's wages. Duncan Murdoch took him on as a clerk when he left school.' He grinned. 'Murdoch wasn't a Scot for nothing. Trust him to take on a lad from an orphanage.'

'An orphanage?' Kelsey echoed with sharp interest.

'St Joseph's, over at Lineholt. It closed down seven or eight years ago. Rising costs — and the feeling's against such places these days, of course.'

Grenville sat back in his chair. 'Foster opened his account with us because his father had had an account here years before.' A very insignificant account; the father had been manager of a small shoe-shop in Cannonbridge until he was called up in the war. He was wounded at Dunkirk, invalided out of the Army. He struggled on for a time in deteriorating health and eventually died of pneumonia following a chill in the grim years after the war, leaving his wife with Gerald, their only child. The widow lost heart and followed her husband in a 'flu epidemic a year or two later.

The boy was passed on to his maternal grandmother. 'She was already an old lady,' Grenville said. 'She didn't have much money—or energy—to bring him up.' She died when Gerald was eleven years old and there was nothing for it then but to send the lad to an orphanage, and the nearest was the one at Lineholt.

But Cannonbridge was always home to Gerald Foster. As soon as he was old enough to think of leaving school and looking for work he turned his eyes to Cannonbridge. He jumped at the chance Murdoch offered.

'Trust Duncan Murdoch to have a shrewd eye for an industrious lad,' Grenville said. A lad with no bad habits of soft living or parental spoiling, no one to rely on but himself, no friends or relatives to encourage him to gad about in search of pleasure.

Foster had certainly grown up to live out the classic dream of industrious orphans of making good by thrift, virtue and hard work—and marrying the boss's daughter.

Whether he then went one further and proceeded to murder the boss's daughter is what I intend to find out, Kelsey told himself grimly as he strode along Market Street back to his car.

Gerald Foster's solicitors, Lawson and Dulcott, was the largest firm of solicitors in Cannonbridge, and by far the busiest. The heavy oak doors closed every evening at five thirty, leaving at least a third of the staff inside to catch up with the paperwork that rose in a fresh tide every morning.

In the late afternoon Sergeant Lambert phoned Mike

Rossiter, the young legal executive who was his contact in the firm. He asked Rossiter if they could meet for a drink.

'I can't get away till half past six,' Rossiter told him.

'That's all right,' Lambert said. 'I'll see you in the White Lion at a quarter to seven.' Rossiter was a bachelor, he lived alone in a flat, was happy to make do with a pint and a sandwich for his evening meal.

He didn't ask Lambert what was in the wind when the sergeant sat down opposite him at a corner table in the White Lion and started asking him questions about Gerald Foster. Rossiter hadn't been all that many years in the legal business but he'd learned enough for that.

He lifted the top of his roast-beef sandwich and inspected the slices of meat with a critical eye. They looked reasonably appetizing. He began to eat with a hearty appetite.

The Fosters' marriage, according to Rossiter, gave every appearance of being stable and satisfactory. Absolutely no hint of any break-up, no threat of divorce, separation, court injunctions. No property disputes, no arguments about finances, personal or business.

Under Mrs Foster's will everything passed to her husband; had Foster died first everything would have gone to Vera. Neither of them had ever expressed any intention of changing the fundamental provisions of either will.

Lawson and Dulcott had been the solicitors of Duncan Murdoch's father, a pawky old Scot whose accent had remained broad till the day he died. He'd been a well-known figure about the streets of Cannonbridge, walking everywhere his business took him, never wasting a penny on a bus fare or — heaven forbid — such a lunatic extravagance as a motor-car.

When he died, Lawson and Dulcott continued as solicitors for his son Duncan; on Duncan's death they remained as solicitors for his daughter Vera. Gerald Foster became their client on his marriage to Vera.

'Absolutely first-rate businessman, Gerald Foster,'
Rossiter said. 'His wife was always too much on the
cautious side. Took after her father and grandfather, no
doubt.' He took a drink of beer. 'What Daddy did and
thought and the way Daddy conducted his business was
by far the best way in Vera's eyes. Daddy's ideas were
sacrosanct.'

'Didn't Foster find that a drag?' Lambert asked. 'Having to pull against her all the time?'

'It never seemed to bother him. He always managed to
talk her into whatever had to be signed. I can't remember
any serious hold-ups on account of her stubbornness.
A few minor delays sometimes, but nothing that really
mattered.'

He took another drink of his beer. 'She was very opposed to a deal he did last spring, a business he bought
dirt-cheap in Lineholt. He really had to talk her into that
one, she was sure he'd never be able to get it going again
on a profitable basis. But she needn't have worried, it's
doing all right.'

Lambert sat back and regarded Rossiter. He got about
a lot, had an adventurous social life, might be expected to
catch the wind of gossip.

'How's Foster with the ladies?' he asked idly.

'He isn't up to tricks,' Rossiter said. 'Nothing like that.
Never a hint.' He gave Lambert a long hard look. 'I'm
just giving you my opinion, of course, but I'd be very
surprised to learn he'd been up to anything.'

And you should be a sound enough judge, Lambert
thought, takes one to know one.

'Business first, last and foremost,' Rossiter said with
conviction. 'That's how Foster always strikes me. Work,
expansion, profits. The next deal. They're the breath of
life to him.'

'Did Vera resent that?'

'Never saw any sign of it. They came into the office

together sometimes. She always seemed rather lovey-dovey, calling him my dear, my love, that sort of thing. Foster took it all good-naturedly enough, he'd pat her hand and smile.'

Doesn't altogether strike me as evidence of deep affection, Lambert thought, seems a good deal more like the insecure kind of relationship where one feels driven to demonstrate the existence of affection—to oneself as much as to outsiders. And Foster's attitude—more like the reassurance one gives a nervous and demanding pet than the loving exchange of equal adults.

'What did you think of Vera?' he asked. 'Did you like her?' Lambert had laid eyes on the lady only after her death. She hadn't looked to him like a mature woman, she had seemed more like an ageing girl, Daddy's chubby little pet, already, at forty, beginning to grow old and grey.

It certainly seemed to fit in with the idea of suicide; the march of the pitiless years must sound like the rolling drums of doom to Daddy's wee flower when the edges of the petals start to turn brown and Daddy is no longer there to offer comfort.

Rossiter finished his sandwich. 'I thought her a twittery sort of creature. The kind to tie strings round you and then try to strangle you with the strings.'

He grimaced. 'All in the name of love, of course.' He drained his glass. 'I'd run a mile from a female like that. I'd find her a right pain in the neck.'

It was well past noon on the following day as Sergeant Lambert walked rapidly along the High Street. He had temporarily forgotten all about Mrs Foster and her untimely death. His mind was occupied with the details of a house-breaking case that had engaged him all morning—with precious little result.

He turned into Bridge Street to cut across an alleyway,

back to the side street where he'd left his car. Several
yards ahead of him a man came out of a doorway, turned
and glanced across the street. Lambert saw that it was
Gerald Foster.

Ah yes — Foster's office was in Bridge Street, Lambert
remembered. He hadn't set foot in the place himself.

Foster didn't see the sergeant, he turned away again
and set off up the street at a good pace.

On an impulse Lambert quickened his own pace and
set off after him. As he passed the doorway that Foster
had come out of, he glanced in at it and saw it was a small
office, the door lettered with the name: Cannonbridge
Thrift Society.

The lower half of the window was of obscure glass;
through the top half Lambert caught a glimpse of iron-
grey corrugations and resolute curls adorning the head of
a lady who must surely be Miss Greatbach, Foster's
secretary and general clerk.

Miss Greatbach stood up and turned to open a drawer
in the filing cabinet behind her. She was stoutly built but
her figure was restrained with rigid discipline. She wore
sober tailored clothes and formidable spectacles; she had
a high, intelligent forehead.

Lambert hastened on. If Master Foster's playing about
with anyone, he thought, I'm prepared to bet my next
two salary increments plus holiday pay, cost-of-living
bonuses and the Christmas club pay-out that his lady-love
is definitely not Madame Greatbach. Unless the vagaries
of the human heart were a good deal more convoluted
than Lambert had so far learned to expect.

He followed Foster through two intersections. A couple
of blocks further on Foster suddenly turned in through a
doorway and vanished. As Lambert came up to the doorway he saw it was a restaurant, a respectable, somewhat
old-fashioned establishment.

Still obeying the same impulse Lambert went inside, up

a flight of stairs and into a dining-room with a subdued clatter of cutlery, hushed voices and potted plants. Venetian blinds filtered out the glare and the worst of the traffic sounds.

Delicious odours of roast beef and apple tart drifted into Lambert's nostrils. He felt a sudden vast appetite.

I'll treat myself to a decent lunch for once, he thought, feeling like a schoolboy out on a treat. It would make a pleasant change from the eternally predictable canteen grub.

He found a table in an alcove near the service area; from here he could observe his quarry while being screened from Foster's view.

Foster sat alone. He was clearly an habitué of the place but he didn't look about him, didn't exchange nods or glances with any of the other diners. He ate resolutely and with despatch, with no sign of relish or appreciation.

Nor did he exchange badinage with the waitress. She was a comely enough girl with a shapely figure and a great deal of fair curly hair under her neat white cap. But for all the attention Foster paid her she might have been the grandmother of the redoubtable Miss Greatbach.

It certainly doesn't look as if he's the readily promiscuous type, Lambert reflected as he embarked on his succulent roast lamb. But that didn't mean that Foster might not be capable of deep and violent passions, in fact it might very well mean exactly that.

When Foster married Vera Murdoch she was presumably still reasonably pretty, reasonably youthful. He could have thought she'd suit him well enough, that he needed no more than she was able to offer.

But then time passed, Foster grew up and matured, he may have discovered that his nature had sides to it he had never so far had time to recognize, let alone explore.

And as Vera grew progressively plainer and more possessively demanding, more irritating and less excusable, Foster might in the course of his business life have come across some woman or girl who seemed to have the potential to satisfy that other side of his nature.

In the first period of his married life he was probably overjoyed at his luck in marrying old Duncan Murdoch's daughter, intrigued by the novelties of married life. The orphan lad must have found the delights of a home of his own — and a fine, well-set-up home at that, with good food, servants, a large garden and all the other comforts — enough to absorb him for some considerable time.

And at first no doubt he would feel that the benefits were rather one-sided, that Vera was bestowing them all on him. He was an orphan and she'd given him a home, he was a town urchin and she'd given him a beautiful country garden, he was a struggling clerk and she'd transformed him into the joint owner of a prosperous well-established business.

But as time wore on it might come to seem to him that the advantages of the union were now being reversed, that it was he who was bestowing the benefits on Vera.

He had vision and enterprise and he was expanding her little cautiously based business; she had inherited a moderate capital and from it he had created much larger assets; she was a woman visibly past her prime and he was still a young and virile man.

He might increasingly come to regard her as a drag on his progress, or, in Mike Rossiter's words, as a right pain in the neck.

Lambert began to eat his portion of delicious treacle tart. Foster had now finished his meal and was drinking coffee while studying the pages of a financial newspaper with care and concentration.

A few minutes later Foster paid his bill and left. Lambert had no doubt but that he'd set off again at a smart pace for his office, to plunge energetically into the afternoon's work.

Lambert began to drink his own coffee. Foster struck him as a solitary man, he certainly didn't behave in everyday life in a friendly and gregarious way. It was easy to see him as a man who might never have married, who might have lived contentedly enough in an austere bachelor flat, scarcely noticing his surroundings, absorbed in building up his business empire.

The thought brought with it an echo of something the Chief had said about Vera Foster. She might never have married, Kelsey had said, but for the chance of her father dying like that, Foster being at hand to assist her through a difficult time. Both of them perhaps essentially single people who had come together by chance.

It hardly seemed a recipe for a happy and satisfying marriage. But it might work well enough on a realistic everyday basis, Lambert reflected as he picked up his bill and walked across to the cash desk.

He came down the flight of stairs into the street and stood on the pavement, considering the duties of the afternoon.

Now that his mind was back on the Foster case he might just take time to slip along to the agency that employed Edith Jordan and see what he could discover about that elegant lady.

CHAPTER 6

The Cannonbridge Staff Agency occupied the ground floor of an old-fashioned office block in a side street near the centre of town.

The agency was owned and run by Miss Unwin, a deceptively frail-looking lady not far off sixty. She gave an impression of softness and prettiness, flowing lines to her clothes, gently waved ash-blonde hair, rose-pink lipstick.

But her eyes were clear and sharp, with a distinct look of being prepared to brook nothing that might compromise the good name of the agency she had founded, had worked long and hard to build up.

Sergeant Lambert disclosed his identity and the fact that he had called to make enquiries about a Miss Edith Jordan.

'I'm sure,' Miss Unwin said pleasantly, 'that you're aware that all our dealings with both clients and staff are wholly confidential. You can surely put your questions to Miss Jordan herself.'

There was a brief silence during which Lambert considered and rejected three or four of his standard replies to such a response; none of them seemed likely to be received by Miss Unwin with more than a look of contempt.

His gaze crossed hers. Her glance was level and direct. He took a chance and spoke the simple truth.

'I don't want Miss Jordan to know that I'm asking these questions at all.'

She gave a little nod as if to say, Yes, that's a perfectly satisfactory answer.

'Before we go any further,' she said crisply, 'you must allow me to ask one or two questions of my own. I am of course aware of the sad circumstances of the death of Mrs Foster during the time Miss Jordan was employed at Lynwood. I can't feel that it's a coincidence that you're here now asking questions about Miss Jordan.'

Lambert opened his mouth to reply but she held up her hand. 'I'm also aware that the verdict on Mrs Foster was that she took her own life. Now — what I am asking you is this: Do you know of any reason why this agency should not continue to employ Miss Jordan?'

Lambert shook his head.

'And if you should become aware of any such reason,' she continued in the same brisk tone, 'do you give me

your word that you will at once inform me? Not of what
you have discovered, I understand of course that that
would be confidential, but of the fact that you have made
such a discovery?'

'I give you my word,' Lambert said. 'And I must
emphasize that we know nothing of any kind whatever
against Miss Jordan from any point of view, personal,
ethical, professional. We have had nothing but the
highest reports of her. I should be very sorry if the fact
that I'm here today should undermine your confidence in
her in any way.'

She gave a single nod. 'Well, then,' she said, leaning
back in her chair, 'let's have your questions.'

Lambert indicated that he wanted to know everything
she could tell him about Edith Jordan, her personal
background, connection with the agency, the length of
time she'd been on its books, how well known she was personally to Miss Unwin or any of her associates, the circumstances in which she had come to be employed at
Lynwood, to what extent Miss Jordan had herself chosen
that particular posting, the references she had produced
on first joining the agency, and the names and addresses
of the last three or four posts she had been sent to before
going to Lynwood.

'Pretty comprehensive enquiries,' Miss Unwin said with
a flash of her grey eyes. But she offered no further objection. She produced files and records.

'Edith Jordan came to us for the first time early this
year,' she said, studying a page. 'On March 1st, to be
exact. She wrote to us in February, giving particulars of
herself and suggesting that we might take her on our
books.

'She gave the names of three referees. We took up two
of her references. They were very satisfactory so we made
an appointment for her to come for an interview. She
came on March 1st and I had a good long chat with her.'

She made a precise little movement of her head. 'We have to be extremely particular. Our ladies go into clients' homes, they hold positions of trust.'

She smiled slightly. 'Miss Jordan impressed me most favourably, I was very pleased to take her on. She said she would like to start work right away so she went out on her first post two days later. There's always a shortage of competent and trustworthy women with a good background; we never have any difficulty in finding the post, it's finding the right woman that's difficult.'

She turned a page in a file. 'We had very good reports of her in her first job. After that we sent her out from job to job in the normal way. She no longer had a home, so she went straight from one job to the next. That isn't uncommon in this type of work, and it was what she wished.'

She looked up at Lambert. 'She told me she intended to work in this way for a year or eighteen months, that she was in fact looking for a small business to buy. She wanted to be able to take her time looking for the right business, and in the meantime agency work would suit her very well.'

'What kind of business is she looking for?' Lambert asked.

'I gather she wants a small business in a good locality, a business that's been allowed to run down so she can buy it cheaply and work to build it up. With living accommodation, of course, she must have that.'

'And the nature of this business?'

'Needlework, wools, embroidery, handmade lingerie, that kind of thing.' Miss Unwin touched the fine gold chain she wore round her neck. 'She's certainly a most accomplished needlewoman. She wears blouses that she makes and embroiders herself, really beautiful work.'

She smiled. 'I'd be very happy to buy such a garment myself if it was to be found in a shop. I'm sure she'll succeed in her venture. She's a woman of capacity, taste and refinement. And there's a demand again for high-class work; people are very tired of the mass-produced.'

She passed across to Lambert the letter Miss Jordan had written when she first approached the agency, together with the replies the agency had received from the two referees.

Miss Jordan's letter was written from the house where she had worked for the previous ten years, an address in Mildenhall, a small town some seven miles to the east of Cannonbridge. The address was printed and the writing paper was of very good quality.

'She was employed there as a companion-nurse,' Miss Unwin said. 'She'd nursed her own mother for some years, then when her mother died she looked for a post requiring some nursing experience. She felt it was work she knew and was good at.'

Lambert studied Edith Jordan's writing, well formed, bold, graceful.

'The Jordan family lived in Mildenhall,' Miss Unwin said. 'The father was an office manager.' She moved her head. 'I got the impression the family had come down somewhat in the world, there might be good blood there somewhere.' She smiled slightly. 'If one is permitted such outdated notions these days. Edith had a reasonably good education, she went to a small boarding school, quite well thought of in its way, over at the other side of the county.

'She was always interested in needlework. When she left school she attended classes in design; I think she had ambitious ideas at that time.

'But her father died suddenly when she was eighteen or nineteen. The mother immediately turned herself into an invalid, you know the sort of thing, took to her bed and abandoned all interest in any kind of new or independent life.' She gave a little snort at the idea of such feminine ineptitude.

'Miss Jordan had to give up her design classes and stay

at home to look after her mother. She imagined this was a purely temporary arrangement, that her mother would soon pull out of her low state and she'd be able to go back to her classes. But the mother never pulled out of it and Miss Jordan never went back to her classes. The mother died fourteen or fifteen years later. She left Miss Jordan what capital she had.'

Lambert ran his eye over the references. The first was from a doctor in Mildenhall who had known Miss Jordan for many years. Her parents had been patients of his and on the death of the mother it was he who had suggested that Miss Jordan might like him to recommend her for the post of nurse-companion to another of his patients, an elderly lady, a Mrs Lydiatt. Miss Jordan had looked after her mother in an exemplary fashion and she had been a faithful employee to Mrs Lydiatt for ten years, until that lady's recent death at an advanced age.

The second reference was from a district nurse in Mildenhall. She had known Miss Jordan personally and professionally for many years, could unreservedly recommend her, and so on, all in terms of unqualified approval.

'And how did Miss Jordan come to be sent to Lynwood?' Lambert asked.

'We supplied Mrs Foster with occasional help from time to time,' Miss Unwin said. 'A temporary cook or general servant, when one of the Lynwood household was ill or on holiday. Then one of her own maids retired earlier this year and wasn't replaced.'

She shook her head. 'It's a problem these days in private service. Anyway—Mrs Foster had one of her bouts of sciatica and was confined to bed. She asked if we could send someone right away, someone with nursing experience to act as general companion-help for a couple of weeks.

'Miss Jordan was just then coming to the end of a

posting. I thought she would do admirably for Lynwood. She started work there right away.

'I phoned Mrs Foster a day or two later to ask if everything was going well — I always do that. She told me she was very pleased with Miss Jordan.'

Miss Unwin gave a small sigh. 'At the time Mrs Foster died so tragically we were expecting to hear from her how much longer she was likely to keep Miss Jordan. After Mrs Foster's death Miss Jordan phoned to say Mr Foster had asked her to stay on till after the funeral, to give a hand generally, as of course there was a great deal of upheaval and extra work. Naturally we agreed at once.

'When it was all over Mr Foster wrote us a very nice letter, saying how much he appreciated all Miss Jordan's help. Then a post came up at a boarding school near here, for a temporary assistant matron. It's a very good school, Orchard House, over at Wychford.

'The post is for the rest of this term, that's a little longer than Miss Jordan usually likes, but she was rather taken with the idea of a boarding school. She enjoyed her own schooldays and she liked the idea of being with so many girls.' She smiled. 'Perhaps it made her feel young again.'

Lambert asked if he might make a note of the last three postings Miss Jordan had gone to before she was sent to Lynwood.

Miss Unwin watched as he wrote down the details. 'I hope she's not in any kind of trouble,' she said as he stood up to leave. 'If there's anything I can do to help her, anything at all, I should be only too pleased.'

Lambert went down the stairs and out into the street. He stood for a moment looking at the list of addresses. None of the places was more than ten miles distant. I'll go over to all three, he decided, I'll have a word with each of her temporary employers.

But today was hopeless, impossible to spare any more time. Tomorrow looked tricky too. He put his notebook away and set off up the street, back to where he'd left his car.

It was three days later before he managed to find the time. In the course of the three days he exchanged no more than a passing word with the Chief about the Foster enquiries; matters a good deal more pressing engaged them both.

Lambert decided to call at the three establishments in the order in which Edith Jordan had worked there. He took a hasty bite of lunch in the canteen and set off immediately afterwards.

At each place he intended to ask the same questions: Had Edith Jordan received any visitors while working there? Any phone calls? Letters? Had she gone out much?

He reached the first place within a few minutes. It was a small detached house near an industrial estate on the outskirts of Cannonbridge. The husband was an invalid, the wife a canteen manageress in a factory on the nearby estate.

The household was normally run by the wife's mother but she had been far from well during the summer and had been ordered by her doctor to take a holiday. Miss Jordan had taken her place for a fortnight.

The mother was now recovered and back in harness. She was able to tell Lambert very little about Miss Jordan except that her daughter had been very satisfied with her; she had not herself met Miss Jordan.

Lambert asked if he might speak to her son-in-law and was shown into a study where a man in early middle age was seated in a wheelchair before a table covered with books and papers.

He seemed surprised that any activities on the part of Miss Jordan should prompt enquiries by the police. He could say with certainty that Miss Jordan had received no visitors during her stay in the house; he would definitely have known if she had.

As far as he was aware the only phone calls she received came from the agency which employed her. He couldn't be sure about the mail but his recollection was that none arrived for her.

Lambert's second call was at a village post office and general store run by a married couple; they had three children of school age. A local woman came in for a few hours every day to help in the house.

During the summer there had been an outbreak of some mild virus infection at the village school. The woman who usually came in to help had stayed at home to nurse her own children. Miss Jordan had worked in the household for ten days. She'd been a godsend, they couldn't have managed without her. In particular they remembered how well she'd got on with the children.

In answer to Lambert's queries about Miss Jordan's mail and other contacts, they were able to be very precise as all mail for the house was delivered to the post office, the telephone was switched through to the shop during the day, and the layout of the premises meant that anyone wishing to reach the living quarters must either walk through the store or pass a window next to the post office counter. Miss Jordan had received no visitors, no mail and no phone calls other than the calls from the staff agency. She had taken no time off while she was there.

Neither husband nor wife expressed any curiosity at the sergeant's visit, being able to snatch only a few minutes from their busy day to answer his questions.

Lambert's final call was at a farmhouse half a mile outside Mildenhall. The farmer's name was Elgood, he and his wife were in late middle age. The farmer's mother lived with them; she was now very old and needed a good deal of attention. The household was normally managed by Mrs Elgood with some casual assistance.

In August Mrs Elgood had slipped while walking across the farmyard and sprained a wrist. She tried to struggle on with her household duties but in the end was compelled to ring the agency.

Miss Jordan worked there for ten days and they thought highly of her abilities. They also liked her personally; she was quiet and self-contained but always courteous and amiable.

'I did ask her to stay on for another week,' Mrs Elgood told Lambert. 'My wrist was more or less better by then but I would have been glad of the extra week. She said she'd like to stay on if it was all right with the agency. I rang them and they agreed. But a couple of days later Miss Jordan told me she'd changed her mind, she'd be leaving at the end of the ten days as we'd originally agreed.'

She pulled a little face. 'So it was straight back to work for me. I managed — after a fashion.'

'Do you know what made her change her mind?' Lambert asked.

'Oh yes, it was the phone call,' she said at once. 'I'm quite sure of that. She got this call and a few minutes later she came looking for me to say she wouldn't be staying on after all. She apologized and said she'd appreciate it if I didn't tell the agency she was the one that had changed her mind, if I'd give them the impression it was me.

'I thought it was probably something personal that had cropped up, I didn't ask her and she didn't explain. Of course I agreed about the agency. She'd been such a help to me, so pleasant and cooperative, it was the least I could do.'

'Have you any idea who the call was from?' Lambert asked. 'Was it you that answered the phone?'

'Yes, I answered it.' She frowned. 'It was a man, that I do remember.'

'Did you ask his name?'

'No, I don't normally do that.'

Miss Jordan had received no other phone calls except those from the agency. She had no mail, no visitors, had taken no time off.

'I shouldn't like to think she's in any kind of trouble.' Mrs Elgood's kindly face creased into an anxious frown.

'Nothing to worry about,' Lambert said vaguely. 'It's really another matter altogether. It only concerns Miss Jordan in a very minor degree.' This seemed to satisfy Mrs Elgood although the sergeant wasn't in the least clear himself what it was supposed to mean.

As he drove back along the narrow lane he pondered what Mrs Elgood had told him. She had been able to say with certainty what day it was that Miss Jordan had received the phone call.

'She told me on the Thursday that she'd be leaving on the Saturday as we'd originally agreed.' Mrs Elgood crossed to a wall calendar and ran a finger along the rows of figures. 'So that makes it August 31st that she told me and September 2nd that she left here.'

So she'd received the phone call on August 31st and next morning she'd rung Miss Unwin at the agency to say she'd be leaving the Elgoods on the following day, and asking if there was another job for her to go to. Miss Unwin told her she'd just had a request for a companion nurse in Abberley village and she thought the post would suit her very well.

It could all tie in, Lambert thought. The man who phoned could have been Foster. If the pair of them were in cahoots they'd probably agreed there should be no contact between them till the time came for Foster to summon Miss Jordan to Lynwood. No meetings, no letters, nothing in the way of damning evidence that could be produced against them later.

All that was necessary was for Miss Jordan to phone Foster each time she changed her address. That would also allow each of them to confirm afresh that the other was still prepared to go along with the scheme.

But it's all speculation, Lambert reminded himself, nothing more than that. He slowed his car to read the signpost at the end of the lane. One arm pointed towards Mildenhall. He stared thoughtfully up at it. It was in Mildenhall that Edith Jordan· had worked for ten years after the death of her mother. Fairhaven, Hawthorn Lane.

He was strongly tempted to call at the house and see if there was anything to be discovered. Not that it's likely, he told himself; Edith Jordan left there seven or eight months ago, I doubt if she's been back since, the present owners may have met her no more than once or twice — if at all.

But all the same he glanced at his watch. I could spare another half-hour, he decided, and turned the car in the direction of Mildenhall.

A few minutes later he halted in front of a small row of shops. A brisk-looking old man came out of the first shop and Lambert asked him for directions.

'Fairhaven's quite near here,' the old man said. He gestured over to his left. 'It's a big house with a very large garden, must be a couple of acres or more. They sold off part of the garden for building after old Mrs Lydiatt died. You can't miss the place, it's got a long garden wall. The house is set well back from the road, up on a rise, you can just see the roof and chimneys from the road.'

Lambert thanked him and got back into his car. Edith Jordan seemed always to have had a rather solitary ex- istence, he mused as he drove along. The years alone with her mother, tied by the demands of the invalid, then ten long years dancing attendance on Mrs Lydiatt, shut away in a secluded house behind high walls.

Even in her temporary posts from the agency, when she might have branched out at last, made new friends, gone out in the evenings, she seemed to have followed the same old pattern, working hard, keeping to herself, never going out to enjoy herself. No wonder she was such an accomplished needlewoman, she must have filled many a long hour practising the craft.

He had a sudden memory of Gerald Foster seated alone at the restaurant table. Speaking to no one, looking neither to right nor left. Two of a kind, perhaps.

He rounded a bend and found himself in Hawthorn Lane. A little way ahead on the right he could see a long high garden wall with a series of landscaped terraces visible above it, banks of ornamental shrubs, a glimpse of chimneys and part of a roof.

He got out of the car. A pair of handsome wrought-iron gates opened on to a drive that wound upwards out of sight. The name on the stone pillars read: Fairhaven.

CHAPTER 7

Lambert walked slowly up the drive, glancing about as he went. Through a gap in the laurel bushes bordering the drive he could see part of the garden. There were a great many tall old trees throwing the long shadows of early autumn. Further on he caught glimpses of a tennis court, thick shrubberies, borders brilliant with dahlias and chrysanthemums. A new-looking fence marked off one section of the land—probably the area of the building site.

As he came in sight of the house he saw a woman walking towards him along a path that led from the rear of the property. She was holding the hand of a small child. The woman was about thirty-five, a fresh-looking pleasant creature; she carried a large, brightly-coloured ball. She gave Lambert a glance of friendly enquiry.

'I'm looking for a Miss Edith Jordan,' he told her.

The woman threw the ball to the child. 'I'm afraid Miss Jordan's not here,' she said amiably. 'It's quite some time since she lived here.'

'It's a business matter,' Lambert said. 'I was given this address.'

'She did work here,' the woman said. 'She was a companion to the lady who used to own Fairhaven. That was a Mrs Lydiatt, she died back in January. Miss Jordan stayed on till the house was sold and the building site disposed of.' She gestured over at the fenced-off area.

'Do you know where Miss Jordan went after she left here?'

'I can give you the address she gave me,' the woman said. 'You're the first person that's called to ask for it.'

She turned and led the way back to the rear entrance. The child ran beside her, clutching the ball.

Lambert followed her into a large old-fashioned kitchen with tall cupboards and open dresser shelves.

'I met Miss Jordan once or twice,' the woman said. 'When we were buying the house.' She opened a dresser drawer. 'This is the address she left.' She took a piece of paper from an envelope and handed it to Lambert.

He unfolded the sheet, knowing what he would see: the address of the Cannonbridge Staff Agency.

'The executors paid Miss Jordan to stay on till the place was sold,' the woman said. 'It doesn't do to leave houses unoccupied these days.'

Lambert handed her back the sheet of paper. 'Did Mrs Lydiatt have any relatives?' he asked casually. 'There must have been a tidy sum to inherit, what with the house and the building site.'

'There must indeed,' she said heartily. 'The site's been sold to a builder. Three detached houses, I understand. They're going to start clearing the ground soon.'

She wrinkled her brow. 'As far as I know there weren't any close relatives. Just some cousins in Australia. I believe they got the bulk of the estate. They put the house on the market right away, through solicitors. I don't suppose any of them had clapped eyes on old Mrs Lydiatt for years — if ever.'

She laughed. 'Of course, I don't know, I'm only guessing. They could have written to her every week for all I know. And flown over to see her every Christmas.'

'Do you know which builder bought the land?' Lambert asked.

She tilted back her head. 'Ormrod. He does a lot of speculative building in this area. He has a good name, nothing cheapjack about his houses.' She laughed again. 'Nor his prices.'

Lambert walked back down the drive and got into his car. Hawthorn Lane continued for a little way and then broadened out into open country. He reversed the car and drove back the way he had come.

When he reached the row of shops again he parked his car and walked along the pavements, glancing in at the premises.

There were three shops; the first was a greengrocer's. Inside, a young man, very tall and thin, with a great deal of dark wavy hair and a moustache that gave him the air of an Oriental bandit, was dragging crates of vegetables from a back area. Hardly the type to exchange confidences with Miss Jordan, Lambert thought.

The next shop was a grocer's. He couldn't see inside as the front windows were heavily plastered with notices set at wild angles to one other and proclaiming with a great many exclamation marks the astonishing array of bargains to be had within.

Lambert stepped inside and pushed his way between rows of shelving that almost prevented his progress, so determined had the shopkeeper been to transform his pygmy premises into a supermarket.

Lambert negotiated the Hampton Court maze of the

shop without encountering a single human eye. As he came up the home straight towards the cash desk, a sulky-looking girl pushed aside a bead curtain and emerged from mysterious regions to one side of the desk.

She gave Lambert a glance of piercing suspicion and hostility. And she's not likely either to have been a bosom mate of Miss Jordan's, Lambert decided. Even if she had been, she scarcely looked disposed now to share her confidences with him.

He snatched a packet at random from a shelf and presented it at the counter. In spite of all the enticing notices on the windows it seemed to Lambert that he was called on to pay a horrifically large sum for such a small packet.

The girl thrust his change at him as if trying to stab him. She uttered not a syllable but managed to imply by her general air of loathing that she was being forced into commercial transactions with some traveller newly returned from the centre of an outbreak of the bubonic plague.

Lambert fought his way into the open air again with the sensation of having escaped from a dense forest. He was astonished to find that outside it was still daylight. He glanced down at the booty in his hand and saw that it was a half-pound packet of cloves.

The last shop was a newsagent's; Lambert went straight in. The shopkeeper and his wife were busy attending to customers but the man gave him a friendly nod and the woman found time to flash a smile at Lambert.

Might do better here, he thought. He amused himself as he waited by twirling a revolving display stand of ladies' tights and panties, and exchanging glances with the saucy young creatures smiling challengingly out at him from the brightly-coloured cellophane wrappers.

When the door pinged behind the last customer Lambert emerged from behind his screen and approached the counter. He bought a box of chocolates — not too large, because he wasn't made of money, but not too small either, as a pursy skinflint wasn't likely to get much in the way of cooperation.

'I wonder if you could help me with a little information,' he said as he paid for his purchase. He was still in his character of harmless member of the public amiably searching for a business contact or an old friend — he still hadn't decided into which category Miss Jordan was about to fall in the present instance.

The shopkeeper gave him a friendly enough look in reply but Lambert saw that the look was edged with the kind of wariness that might greet duns, divorce enquiry agents, local authority inspectors and other enemies of the people.

'I'm trying to find out the whereabouts of an old friend,' he said, instantly settling on Miss Jordan's category. The shopkeeper's face relaxed somewhat. 'A Miss Edith Jordan,' Lambert added, encouraged by this softening.

He saw at once that the name was known to them. 'She worked for some years up at Fairhaven, in Hawthorn Lane,' he said, 'for a Mrs Lydiatt. I now discover that Mrs Lydiatt has passed on, the house has been sold, and Miss Jordan is no longer living round here. I wonder if you happen to know where she's gone.'

'It was ever so sad about Mrs Lydiatt,' the woman said with ready good nature. 'Quite a shock it was to poor Miss Jordan, though not a surprise to us really, Mrs Lydiatt was an invalid for years. But you get used to things, you think they'll never change, and when you're fond of someone it's always a shock when they go. Miss Jordan looked after Mrs Lydiatt ever so well, she couldn't have done more for her if she'd been her daughter.'

Lambert murmured and shook his head with an expression of generalized sorrow and understanding.

'Miss Jordan used to come in here regularly,' the woman went on. 'For magazines and sweets and so on, for Mrs Lydiatt. Very quiet lady, Miss Jordan, very reserved and refined, kept very much to herself, never mixed locally, if you understand me. But always polite and civil. I liked her.'

'She was looking for another job after Mrs Lydiatt died,' the newsagent said. 'There was a nice piece about the funeral in the local paper. She came in for the paper and I mentioned what a nice write-up it was. I asked if she'd made any plans about her future and she told me she'd agreed to stay on till the property was sold and then she'd be looking for another job, similar to the one she had at Fairhaven. She didn't think it would take long to find something to suit her but she didn't expect it to be round these parts. She thought that would be too much to hope for, but she ought to be able to find something in the same county.'

'We didn't see much of her after that,' his wife said. 'I didn't get a chance to say goodbye, you know how it is at the end, it's always a rush when you leave anywhere. I'm afraid I can't give you her address, I don't know where she went.'

Lambert left the shop as half a dozen children swarmed in. He got back into his car and looked at his purchases. He knew it would shortly be his landlady's birthday. On that milestone day she would be sixty and officially entitled to a retirement pension, as well as to a controlled amount of free joy-riding on the local buses, half-price fines for overdue books at the library, and the senior-citizen-size (a weighty term meaning small) portion of fried fish at the local chip shop.

Lambert was aware of these facts because the good lady had mentioned one or other or all of them to him on average twice a week over the last few months, sometimes with resigned expectation but more often with vociferous contempt.

He put the packages on the dashboard shelf. In two days' time, he thought, guess who's going to be delighted to receive, in addition to all those bureaucratic joys, a five-hundred-gram box of chocolates and an eight-ounce packet of whole cloves.

As he set the car in motion a horrid thought struck him. He had hitherto marked his landlady's birthday only with a brief expression of verbal good wishes when he caught sight of the array of festive cards on the mantel-piece. She would be surprised, not to say astounded, at this sudden change in tactics.

I hope she's not going to start reading something into it, he thought with deep foreboding. Wiser perhaps to forget the birthday offerings, play safe, stick to the oral greetings. His tastes, even in times of deprivation and near-desperation, didn't run to mauve rinses and garden-fencing corsets.

Two days later—and a busy, crowded two days, working late and achieving little, with no time to spare a thought for the Foster case—Lambert was returning to the station at the end of an afternoon spent in maddeningly fruitless enquiries into an outbreak of vandalism on an outlying housing estate.

The last of the sunlight lingered over the station forecourt as he stepped out of his car. He was halfway across the forecourt when he saw Chief Inspector Kelsey come out through the main doors.

The Chief glanced over at Lambert as he came down the steps. He paused and frowned, looked at his watch and then stood impatiently waiting for the sergeant to reach him.

'Where have you been?' Kelsey said sharply as Lambert came up. Lambert told him briefly. The Chief grunted and looked again at his watch. 'The Foster business,' he said. 'Done anything on that?'

'Quite a bit,' Lambert said.

The Chief made a sucking noise with his tongue. He glanced across at his car. 'All right,' he said suddenly. 'Another twenty minutes won't hurt.' He turned and began to stride back up the steps with Lambert bounding behind him.

Back inside the building the Chief waved aside a constable who tried to speak to him. He went rapidly along to his own room with Lambert in his wake.

'Right, then,' Kelsey said as soon as they were inside the room. 'Start talking. Everything you've found out so far.'

He listened intently as Lambert sketched an account of his doings. He was particularly interested in Lambert's conversation with Miss Unwin at the Cannonbridge Staff Agency.

'This business Edith Jordan talks of buying,' he said when Lambert paused to draw breath. 'How's she proposing to finance the purchase? Building society mortgage? Bank loan?'

'I don't know.'

'Find out,' Kelsey said briskly.

'She may be thinking of paying cash,' Lambert said. 'She could have a fair bit of capital. She inherited whatever her mother left. If she invested that at the time it could have increased considerably by now. And she must have been left something by Mrs Lydiatt, possibly a good deal. She was there ten years and they seem to have got on well. I imagine Miss Jordan's the type to save her wages, invest them wisely. I gather she was well paid at Fairhaven. All in all, she could have quite a tidy sum behind her by now.'

Kelsey performed some elaborate facial exercises. 'She certainly doesn't give any indication of reckless spending or extravagant tastes,' he said. She struck him as a woman of austere personal habits. He continued to contort his craggy features as Lambert described his visits to Edith

Jordan's last three employers.

'There doesn't seem to be much to go on,' Lambert observed. 'Her behaviour at all those places seems to have been exactly what might be expected.' The more he heard of Edith Jordan the less likely it seemed that she could be the object of passionate attentions from any man — least of all from Gerald Foster.

And she seemed to like the work she did, the life she led, he had heard nothing to make him suspect she was unhappy with her lot, basically discontented, desperately searching for a way out. 'Are you quite sure,' he said mildly, 'that you're not barking up the wrong tree?'

'I'm not in the least sure.' Kelsey passed a hand across his face; it did little to smooth out his features. 'It's highly likely that I'm barking up the wrong tree. But it can't be helped.'

His nature simply wouldn't permit him to forget the whole thing, put it out of his mind and get on with tackling the housebreakings and the vandalism, let Vera Foster sleep in the tranquil earth beneath the yew trees in Abberley churchyard.

'I shall continue barking up this particular tree,' he said, 'until it becomes blindingly clear that the tree is empty. And what is more,' he added with ferocity, 'you will continue to bark up it too.'

Lambert moved his shoulders in a manner that indicated acceptance, resignation, and the fact that he had never really expected any other response.

'And another thing,' the Chief said suddenly, 'these two legacies Edith Jordan received. Or is said to have received. Exactly how much did each amount to?'

'I don't know.'

Kelsey stabbed the air a few inches from Lambert's nose. 'Find out. And when you've found out, check it. And then check it again.'

He closed his eyes briefly. Check everything, he was

always telling them. As soon as you hear of a so-called fact, check it. Even if you think you already know the answer, check it. Most particularly check it then, that's when the pit opens and you drop inside if you're not doubly careful. And still they let things slip past them.

As soon as Kelsey woke up each morning his first thought was always to establish what day of the week it was. Sometimes this took him several seconds. When he was satisfied he'd got it right he glanced at the clock, which carried the date and day of the week as well as the time, to confirm that what he had worked out was correct. Ninety-nine times out of a hundred he would be right.

But there was always that hundredth time when he'd been absolutely sure he'd got it right—and he'd got it wrong.

'I can't find any connection between Foster and Edith Jordan before she went to Lynwood,' Lambert said. And this connection was surely what they were looking for, the cornerstone of the Chief's theory. 'There's just the possibility that the man who phoned her at the Elgoods could have been Foster.' But they could never establish that now.

Kelsey waved a hand. 'Get on with the rest of it. What else did you find out?'

Lambert told him about his visit to Fairhaven and what he'd learned of Edith Jordan's years with Mrs. Lydiatt.

'She stayed on after the funeral,' he said. 'At the request of the executors. The bulk of the estate went to relatives in Australia. They put the house and the piece of land on the market—'

'Piece of land?' Kelsey said sharply.

'There's a big garden at Fairhaven. Must be a couple of acres altogether. None of the Australian lot intended coming over here, they left it all to be handled by local solicitors and so on. The garden was split up, the greater part was put on sale as a building plot.'

'Why did they want Edith Jordan to stay on?'

'To prevent the house standing empty. And to show prospective purchasers round.'

Kelsey struck the desk. 'There's your connection! Foster saw the land advertised. He went over to inspect it, met Edith Jordan, she showed him over the site. He probably went over to Fairhaven more than once, making his mind up about the land.'

'And he immediately said to her,' Lambert couldn't refrain from saying, 'By the way, when you've finished here at Fairhaven, would you be willing to come over to Lynwood—not right away, but say in six or nine months, and assist me to make away with my wife?'

Kelsey gave a laugh. 'I'll bet that was the gist of it, even if it was more subtly wrapped up and took longer than five minutes to get down to.'

He tilted back his chair. 'Foster was probably fed up with Madame Vera for a long time before he set foot in Fairhaven.' Easy enough for a man in Foster's situation, with Foster's temperament, to look at a dependent, ageing hypochondriac like Vera, a woman with the power to act as a drag on all his plans, easy enough for such a man to feel: What earthly use is such a creature to anyone? Who would be a ha'porth worse off if she vanished from the face of the globe? Such a train of thought might well by slow and resentful degrees slide into a fancied justification for murder.

'I don't know if there was much affection on Foster's side when he married Vera,' Kelsey said, 'but my guess is there was precious little affection left by the time he went over to Fairhaven.'

He banged the legs of his chair down on the floor. 'All he wants by the time he meets Edith Jordan is to keep the benefits of his marriage with none of the drawbacks.'

'Why not just get a divorce?' Lambert said. 'Five years

apart without consent.' Hard to imagine Vera being cooperative enough in such a matter to agree to divorce by consent after two years' separation.

Kelsey shook his head. 'You've answered yourself. Foster couldn't even start proceedings for five years. Can you imagine what those five years would be like for him? Trying to run the business with Vera full of resentment because he's walked out on her, ready to take any steps to revenge herself. Using every one of her legal powers to hinder, delay, frustrate and hamper. She'd probably bring the firm to the verge of bankruptcy long before the five years were up. Foster certainly couldn't pursue his policy of expansion, calculated risk.

'And even if he did manage to keep the business afloat till the divorce, the financial settlement would pretty well fleece him. Everything would be split down the middle. If anything, Vera would get more than a half share, possibly a good deal more. After all, the house and the original business were entirely hers. She could probably claim all that, plus one half of the rest—whatever Foster had added to the business since he married her. That would clip Master Gerald's wings very neatly. He could be left singing for his supper. I very much doubt he'd care for that way out.'

Foster didn't strike the Chief as a man to endure with patience the delays, manipulations, artificially arranged disputes and all the other devices of lawyers intent on dragging out a case in order to wear down the opposition and obtain the largest possible settlement by a species of legalised harassment and blackmail.

'All right,' Lambert said. 'Divorce isn't on.'

'Foster starts to toy with various ideas of freeing himself,' Kelsey said. 'He eventually comes round to pondering the notion of doing away with her, probably only as a fanciful piece of fantasy at first, and then a little more seriously. But as soon as he gives it any serious consideration he sees at once that suspicion must always point the finger straight at him. But what if he could somehow not be there when she breathes her last? Then it might be feasible. He remembers Vera's early attempt at suicide. That's an idea he can start to build on.

'But he can't do it alone, he needs an ally. He broods on the idea, keeps coming back to it, it's never far from his mind.'

Yes, I could see Foster as an obsessive type, Lambert thought.

'Then he meets Edith Jordan,' Kelsey said. 'She shows him over the building plot. They chat, she tells him her employer is dead, she is now out of a job, she will soon be out of a home. Foster begins to feel she could be the person he's looking for. A woman he could come to terms with, cool, efficient, unemotional. And she's been a companion-nurse—exactly the kind of ally he needs.

'He comes to see her again, starts to sound her out. When he sees she's beginning to catch on, she isn't horrified, doesn't at once reject his suggestions, he's able to be a little more specific, and then again a little more, until at last it's all out in the open, it's agreed between them in principle, they can get down to planning it all in detail.' His forehead shone damply, he pulled a handkerchief from his pocket and dabbed at it.

'But we've no reason to suppose Foster ever went to Fairhaven, ever laid eyes on the building plot,' Lambert objected.

'We'll soon find that out,' Kelsey said robustly. 'It's exactly the sort of thing Foster would be interested in. You ask, you'll find out he bought the land.'

'But I have asked,' Lambert said. 'I did find out who bought the land. It definitely wasn't Gerald Foster.'

Kelsey was brought to an abrupt halt. 'You're sure of this?'

'Absolutely certain. Ormrod bought it, the builder.

The woman at Fairhaven told me about it. Ormrod's putting three houses on the site. He's going to start clearing the ground any day now.'

'No doubt about it?' Kelsey said with fierce disappointment.

'No doubt at all.'

Kelsey stared moodily at Lambert. There was a silence, broken a few moments later by a knock at the door—the Chief's presence urgently sought elsewhere.

Kelsey got to his feet and looked across at Lambert. 'I'm still barking.' He grinned. 'Not very loudly perhaps, but make no mistake, I'm still in there barking.'

A day or two later on a fine, clear morning Lambert was on his way back to Cannonbridge from a call at a hospital in connection with an accident involving a stolen car. He was still some distance from Cannonbridge when he found himself forced to pull into the side of the road to allow passage to a large lorry that was trying to manœuvre itself through the entrance to a site where machines were at work amid a deafening clatter.

Lambert sat waiting in his car, thinking over the interview at the hospital. Then he grew impatient and stuck his head out of the window.

Above the hedge at the other side of the road a board proclaimed: Ormrod Construction Ltd.

He got out of his car and walked over to where the site foreman stood watching the lorry driver's operations with an expression of dubious appraisal. Lambert asked if the gaffer was anywhere about.

The foreman gave him a suspicious glance and Lambert introduced himself. 'I just want a word,' he said in tones of strong reassurance, knowing the jumpy nature of building foremen in the presence of the law. 'Won't keep him a moment. Some information I want about a building plot he bought. Nothing to worry about.'

'As a matter of fact he's here on the site,' the foreman said after another moment's pondering. He glanced over his shoulder. 'Back there.'

Lambert made his way over the rough ground to where a half-built dwelling gaped at the sky. He discovered Ormrod—a short, thickset man with brilliant blue eyes and a tanned face seamed with wrinkles—at the rear of the house. He was squatting on his haunches, examining with an expression of marked distaste a consignment of joinery. Lambert had to crouch down beside him and shout in his ear.

'Yes, yes, what is it you want?' Ormrod said with irritation when it had got through to him who Lambert was. One of the lads been nicking something again, was the thought that ran clearly across his lizard face.

Lambert managed to persuade him to stand up and walk over to a comparatively quiet spot where a couple of tall and very ugly old trees—designated by the local council as of inestimable artistic value and so to be preserved for posterity, to the fury of the builder who found them ceaselessly and expensively incommoding—provided some shelter from the clatter.

As soon as he was upright and no longer faced with the substandard joinery Ormrod's manner grew markedly less irritable. He lit a cigarette and drew a deep breath of satisfaction.

'Well, then,' he said. Lambert asked him about the Fairhaven site.

'Oh, that one,' Ormrod said. 'Nice little spot. Should be starting work there by the end of the month. If the weather holds.'

Yes, he had definitely bought the site, had completed the purchase. And yes, he did buy the site from the executors of the late Mrs Lydiatt. He mentioned a firm of estate agents with branches all over the county, long established and highly reputable.

'I dealt with the Cannonbridge branch. And not too fancy a price either, between you and me.' He drew on his cigarette. 'They wanted it all cleared up quickly. Suited me, I'm not one to hang about if there's business to be done.'

He showed no curiosity about the reason for Lambert's questions. Once he was satisfied neither he nor his men were suspected of misdeed he seemed not to care tuppence what else might be in the wind.

He walked with Lambert down to the road. His manner was relaxed now, cheerful and friendly. 'I'll have to be getting across to one of my other sites,' he said. 'See what kind of horrible mess they're making of the job over there.' He grinned. 'The thing I like about this life, you're always in one hell of a mess.' He seemed to find it exhilarating.

He stood watching as Lambert got into the car. The lorry had by now discharged its load; the foreman was signing the driver's papers.

'You'll be able to pull out in a moment,' Ormrod said. He stuck his head in at the window and said on a reflective note, 'Yes, nice little site, Mildenhall. Very pleased with it.' He winked at Lambert. 'But then Foster's a pretty shrewd judge. Doesn't often let me down.'

CHAPTER 8

Lambert experienced a sensation as of having been struck in the stomach by a cricket ball. 'Foster?' he echoed.

'Yes, Gerald Foster. Cannonbridge Thrift. Good judge of a piece of land.'

'What did he have to do with the Mildenhall site?'

'It was Foster tipped me the wink. That's enough for me, I don't need telling half a dozen times. Not the first time he's put me on to a good site, he keeps his ear to the ground. If he gives me the nod I look sharp about it, snap it up before anyone else does, I know it won't be some rubbishy slag-heap.'

He grinned. 'He scratches my back, I scratch his. Piece of land he hears about, decides he doesn't want, thinks might suit me, he gives me a buzz.' He paused. 'Nasty business that, about his wife.' He shook his head. 'Middle-aged women, they go into these depressions, I've known one or two cases.' He shook his head again and blew out a long breath.

'Yes, indeed,' Lambert said. He allowed a moment or two to pass in silence then he said in an idle tone, 'Had Foster been to see the site? Been over himself to view it?'

Ormrod was watching the lorry driver pull away. 'I imagine so,' he said. 'That's the usual drill.'

'But you don't know so?' Lambert felt obliged to persist.

'No, I don't actually know so.' Ormrod's eyes still followed the driver's manoeuvres. 'Foster rang through to my office, left a message, I rang the agent, skipped over right away, bought it, rang Foster and said, Ta very much. Good building sites don't turn up every day of the week. Half of those that do have got no end of snags attached. Covenants and God knows what.'

He frowned suddenly, took his eyes off the lorry and darted a keen glance at Lambert. 'What do you want to know for?'

'No particular reason.' Lambert allowed a note of boredom to colour his tone. 'Just wondered why Foster didn't buy the site himself. Seeing the price was so reasonable.'

Ormrod looked reflective. 'I don't know, didn't ask him. Must have had some reason.' He moved his shoulders. 'No concern of mine. I make my own decisions, I let other folk worry about why they make theirs.'

Lambert risked one final observation. 'That would be Miss Jordan that showed you over the site?'

Ormrod looked puzzled. 'Miss Jordan? I don't know any Miss Jordan. I rang the agent, he took me over, I didn't see anyone else.' He stood back to let Lambert move off.

Ormrod turned his head to look up the road and caught sight of a car pulling up some yards away. Sitting beside the driver was an official from the local planning department.

Ormrod gave Lambert a perfunctory wave and darted off to speak to the man. By the time Lambert had reached the main road Ormrod had forgotten all about the sergeant and his questions.

I never did phone London about those two wills, Lambert remembered as he turned the car towards Cannonbridge; Kelsey would soon be demanding details of the legacies Edith Jordan was supposed to have received.

That meant a few local calls first to get precise details, names, dates and so on. He made a mental note to deal with it as soon as he entered the station.

And another thing Kelsey had told him to ferret out and he'd totally forgotten shot up now into the forefront of his mind—the steps Edith Jordan was taking to find herself a suitable little business, how she proposed to finance the purchase.

The Chief Inspector was away for a couple of days, attending a conference. He'd expect all this information to be ready and waiting for him when he got back.

Lambert began to feel the old familiar surge of interest. Until now he hadn't been able to treat the Chief's barkings very seriously. But it had taken just that one little moment, Ormrod sticking his head in at the car window, looking down at him with casual matiness, saying, Shrewd chap, Foster, sound judgment, good eye for a piece of land.

It may still be nothing but moonshine, he reminded himself sternly as he caught sight of his face in the driving-mirror, recognizing that look, the dog on the scent.

Foster might never have seen the building plot, may never have been anywhere near Fairhaven, could have learned of the site in a dozen different ways, could have had as many good reasons for not being interested in it himself, might simply have decided to pass the word on to Ormrod in the usual way.

By the time he reached Cannonbridge the glow had begun to fade. It did indeed begin to look like moonshine — but he would all the same make his phone calls and then have a bite to eat.

He had just come up from the canteen when he had a call from the Lineholt police. They'd picked up a lad earlier in the morning, hanging round a motorway service station, trying the doors of cars. He was half-starving, looked as if he'd been sleeping rough. He would give no account of himself, stubbornly refused to say anything at all, but his appearance roughly fitted the description of a lad who'd vanished some days before from his foster-home in Cannonbridge, taking with him the few pounds his foster-mother had in her purse.

Lambert knew the boy, who'd been in minor trouble before. 'I'll come over right away,' he told the inspector. Half an hour later he walked up the steps of the Lineholt police station. One look at the closed, defiant face of the youngster in custody told him the lad was a total stranger.

The inspector was a genial man coming to the end of his time in the force. 'Sorry you had a wasted journey,' he told Lambert. He came out on to the steps and stood chatting about the changes he had seen over the years, the frightening rise in juvenile delinquency, the difficulties of dealing with disturbed youngsters in a society itself full of turmoils and upheavals.

'Things were a good deal more straightforward in the old days,' he said. 'I dare say they weren't any better but they were certainly simpler.' He reminisced about the ways of the old juvenile courts and borstals.

'All this fostering,' He pursed his lips. 'In some ways I suppose it's a good thing, more informal, nearer normal family life, but there isn't the discipline there was in the old orphanages and children's homes.' He shook his head. 'They're all gone now of course—or going. Take St Joseph's, five hundred boys they used to have there. All run by private charity, didn't cost the taxpayer a penny. Most of the lads turned out very well, we hardly ever had one of them through the courts.'

St Joseph's, Lambert thought, surely that was where Gerald Foster spent five or six years of his adolescence.

'Pulled down now,' the inspector said with another shake of his head. 'Didn't fit into the modern scheme of things. They put up a housing estate on the land. Half of it's no longer fit to live in—hooligans and vandals.'

Lambert asked if he knew what had happened to the staff when St Joseph's closed down.

'There weren't many of them left by that time,' the inspector said. 'They'd been running it down for the last few years. The younger men found jobs in local authority homes, the rest retired. Old Weaver, the deputy superintendent, he still lives round here. He gave his whole life to St Joseph's.'

Lambert drew him out about Weaver. 'He still takes an interest in youth work.' The inspector grinned. 'He walks round the town every day, rain or shine. Holds himself like a ramrod, shoes you could see your face in, always a fresh flower in his buttonhole. This time of day he'll be sitting in the rose garden by the monument, in the shelter if it's raining, you could set your watch by him.'

The monument was a granite memorial to the first world war standing in a pretty little square near the centre of Lineholt. The rose garden, still with late roses blooming in the neat beds, was well provided with seats. Among the half-dozen pensioners chatting and reading it was easy to pick out Weaver sitting erect on his bench, a carmine rosebud in his lapel.

Lambert sat down beside him and made an observation about the glorious weather. Weaver at once began to talk, eagerly, with animation, as if starved of conversation. Must be lonely for him after the crowded years at St Joseph's, Lambert thought.

Within a few minutes Weaver had—without prompting—given Lambert an outline of his career, described his sorrow when St Joseph's closed down, indicated his current schemes for filling the long days.

'I'm a widower,' he said. 'My wife died fifteen years ago. She was one of the best.' He drew a long trembling breath. 'We were never fortunate enough to have children of our own, she mothered all the lads at St Joseph's, they were her whole life.' Tears sparkled in his eyes. 'When she died it was in all the local papers, and the county gazette. Over two hundred old boys came back for the funeral. There were boys working in London and Birmingham and even a couple from Scotland that came. And I had letters afterwards from Canada and Australia, they'd all heard.'

He lived in digs now. His landlady was kind enough, competent enough, but it wasn't the same. 'She doesn't like me staying in the house during the day, I've got in the habit of being out all the time. I don't mind it now but at first—' He sighed and shook his head.

He displayed no curiosity about Lambert apart from one shrewd glance in the first few minutes, followed by a smiling comment. 'I'm a good judge of men, pride myself on it. I'll wager I can guess what you do for a living. Local government—now I'm not far wrong, am I?'

'Spot on,' Lambert said. 'Over in Cannonbridge.'

Weaver wasn't interested in Cannonbridge. All his interest was in Lineholt, St Joseph's, the boys, memories of the old days.

Lambert decided he could introduce Foster's name without finesse.

'I was talking to a chap some time back,' he said. 'Name of Foster, Gerald Foster. He mentioned he'd been at St Joseph's—must be twenty years ago or thereabouts.'

'Gerald Foster,' Weaver said at once. 'Thin little chap, looked as if he carried the world on his shoulders. I remember him all right.' He laughed. 'Only boy I ever knew to get money out of old Colonel Branderby.'

He saw Lambert's look of interest. 'The boys used to get pocket-money every week, not much, of course, and most of them spent it the moment they laid hands on it, but Foster put his away every week in the post office, never spent a single penny of it that I could ever make out. When the boys left St Joseph's they were always given ten pounds to help them on their way—the money came from an endowment by a wealthy patron way back. In those days they always had a job to go to and we'd got their digs all fixed up for them, we never sent a lad out without making proper arrangements. The ten pounds was a little bonus, a farewell gift.

'Anyway, when the time came for Foster to leave he had over thirty pounds saved up, not a bad little sum for those days. Colonel Branderby decided he didn't need the ten pounds and I was given the job of telling Foster.' He laughed again, with a note of admiration. 'I never knew he could look so fierce. He was always a very quiet lad, never any trouble. He didn't say a word when I told him, but he looked plenty. He went straight off and sat down and wrote the Colonel a letter. He didn't show it to me, didn't tell me he was writing it but the Colonel showed it to me afterwards, it made a powerful impression on him. All about how they were penalizing thrift and forethought and self-discipline, the very qualities they were supposed to be trying to teach the boys. There were a couple of pages of it, very impassioned stuff.'

He laughed aloud. 'The upshot was he not only got his ten pounds but the Colonel gave him another ten out of his own pocket—in front of all the lads, made a regular speech about it.' He smiled in pleased reminiscence.

He glanced at Lambert. 'You don't happen to know what he's doing these days?'

'Some line of development business,' Lambert said vaguely. 'We didn't have much of a chat, but he seemed prosperous enough.'

'He never came back to see us after he left,' Weaver said. 'Not once.'

'Did that surprise you?'

'Not really. I was disappointed but not altogether surprised. He was never what you'd call friendly, never had any close mates. Self-sufficient, always had an air of being full of plans, knowing exactly where he was going. After the early days, that is, he took some time to settle in. He was very quiet at first, withdrawn, almost, no trouble, very obedient but shut in on himself. My wife tried everything she could think of to get him to cheer up and join in with the others. Then after a few weeks he seemed to settle in all at once as if he just made up his mind to it. Some of the lads we got—' he shook his head and sighed—'very disturbed, broken homes, every kind of ill-treatment. We had a terrible job with some of them. That was where my wife was so good.' He stared ahead at the roses. 'She did wonders with them.'

He glanced at Lambert. 'There's a lad now in the local infirmary, an old St Joseph's boy, name of Dalby. I called in to see him yesterday. He works on a farm about ten miles from here. He had an accident on his motor-bike, broke both his legs. He'd be much the same age as Foster, now I come to think of it. Dalby came from a very bad background. His mother was widowed and they were very badly off. She married again—out of desperation, I fancy, as much as anything, trying to keep the home together. The step-father bullied that lad half out of his mind. In the end the mother took ill and died and the lad came to us.

'I thought we'd never get him to cheer up or take an interest. He was frightened of everybody, flinched if you made a sudden movement, spent most of his time crying, wouldn't eat, couldn't sleep. But my wife got him round in the end. He was as happy a lad as you'd wish to meet before he left, turned out to be one of our best cricketers—not like Foster. Foster never went in for sport, no more than he was forced to. I did everything to get him interested but it was no use.'

He laughed. 'He said to me: I don't care for pointless activity. He'd no time for hobbies, either. Carpentry, metalwork, some of the lads turned out lovely stuff. Dalby made a fruit bowl for my wife, beautiful job, marquetry. I've got it now in my digs. Dalby was very attached to my wife. He came to see us regularly after he left, brought a great sheaf of white lilies to her funeral.'

He looked at the yellow roses, brave in the sunshine, then he said briskly, 'Which reminds me—I promised to look out some books for Dalby. I help with the Scouts, they collect waste paper and we often get paperbacks in among it. I sort out the best and take them along to the infirmary. Dalby was always a great reader.' He stood up. 'I'll get along to the hut now and sort through the books, I promised to take him some next week.'

Lambert got to his feet. 'I'll come along with you if I may, I'm at a bit of a loose end for an hour or two.'

'Glad of your company,' Weaver said heartily.

Ten minutes' walk through the shopping centre, past a housing estate and down a side road brought them to a stoutly built hut standing on a patch of neatly tended land.

'Belongs to the Council,' Weaver said as he produced a key and unlocked the door. 'They let us have it at a nominal rent.'

The interior of the hut was scrupulously clean and tidy. On a long trestle table waste paper of various kinds had been separated into piles, one of them a stack of paperbacks. Weaver began to glance through them. After a few moments he uttered a sound of disgust. 'Of course we don't take anything like this up to the infirmary.' He held out a book with a cover showing a young woman in a torn slip backing away from a hooded figure brandishing a whip.

Lambert helped to look through the books and they built up a little pile of biographies and memoirs, detective novels, thrillers, stories of wartime escapes. Weaver separated half a dozen for Dalby.

'I'll drop them in at the infirmary if you like,' Lambert offered. 'I have to go out that way, it wouldn't be any trouble.'

'That's very good of you.' Lambert took the books. 'Tell Dalby,' Weaver added, 'this lot's just to be going on with, we'll be getting another lot of sacks in on Friday.' He looked at his watch. 'I've one or two jobs to do while I'm here, then I'll have to be getting back for lunch.'

He walked with Lambert to the door. Around the walls photographs of boys were arranged in ranks, boys in uniform, in athletic gear, marching, camping, playing musical instruments.

'I've enjoyed our chat.' Weaver shook hands warmly. He stood looking out at the bright sunlight.

'What did hurt about Foster,' he said suddenly, 'what I really couldn't understand, was he never came to her funeral, never sent flowers, didn't so much as write a letter. And she'd been so good to him.'

CHAPTER 9

The infirmary was a cluster of old-fashioned red-brick buildings on the lines of a cottage hospital. Lunch was already over when Lambert walked up to the reception desk.

Yes, certainly he could go up and have a short visit with Mr Dalby; he was doing well, would probably be glad of a chat.

Dalby was in a little side ward. Both his legs were in plaster, supported by an arrangement of hoists. He had a bandage round his head and pieces of sticking-plaster on his face. He was lying back with his eyes closed, listening to the radio.

He was delighted to see a visitor, particularly one carrying books. He glanced through them as Lambert explained he'd been chatting to Weaver, had offered to drop the books in.

'Sit down if you've got a minute,' Dalby said and Lambert pulled up a chair. Dalby was a powerful-looking young man with a tanned face and thickly springing black hair sprouting above his bandage. A vigorous growth of curly black hair showed at the neck of his pyjama jacket.

'Decent chap, old Weaver,' he said. 'I expect you heard the story of his life.'

'And the history of St Joseph's. I found it very interesting.' It took Lambert no more than another couple of minutes to work Foster's name into the conversation via Weaver's anecdote about the ten-pound leaving present.

'Gerald Foster,' Dalby said. 'I haven't seen him since the day he left. I bet he's done all right for himself, he'll probably end up a millionaire.' He looked at Lambert.

'He used to make a book on all the classic races, used to study form. He never clapped eyes on a racehorse in the flesh, never set foot on a racecourse, but he read all the racing pages. There were always plenty of newspapers at St Joseph's, the staff left them lying about, he read them all.'

He gestured at the pile of paperbacks. 'He wouldn't give you tuppence for books like those, thought they were a waste of time. All the lads had a bet with him, three-pence or fourpence, Foster always made money from it. Weaver would have had a fit if he knew, he thought Foster was a pillar of virtue.'

He laughed. 'Foster bet me five shillings once, that was a terrific sum. I was running away—we weren't badly treated or anything like that but I was always reading adventure stories, I had my head full of romantic rubbish. I got it into my head I'd escape, I was going to make for London. God knows what I thought I'd do when I got there. Foster bet me I wouldn't make it.'

'He wasn't tempted to join you?'

'Not he! "Bet you five bob you don't get as far as Reading," he said when I told him, that was all he was interested in. I knew he wouldn't shop me, you could rely on him to keep his mouth shut.'

He grinned. 'I didn't get farther than thirty miles. It was a fine dry morning when I set off but it clouded over later on and by the afternoon it was teeming down. It poured all night and all next day. I lay up in a barn but not before I'd got soaked to the skin. I got a bad chill and when it did clear up next day I felt so rotten I knew I wouldn't be able to go on. I walked up to a vicarage and asked them to ring St Joseph's. One of the masters came over in a car to fetch me. I was in the sick bay for ten days.'

'Did Foster let you off the five bob?'

'He did not. He made me pay up. I'd no money left,

not a penny, and I didn't get any pocket money for three months afterwards. He just waited till I did get some. He didn't mind waiting.'

'If you had made it to London and won your bet,' Lambert said with curiosity, 'would you have expected Foster to pay you your five bob?'

'Yes, of course. We fixed that. I was to drop him a line to let him know where to send it. He'd have paid all right, he was never a welsher.'

He stared thoughtfully at Lambert. 'I only ever saw him cry once, all the time he was at St Joseph's. A lot of the boys used to cry at night under the bedclothes, especially when they first came, the young ones particularly. There was a dog, an old dog that belonged to the chap that stoked the boilers. Foster made a pet of it, it used to wait for him, follow him round.

'One night it got out on to the road, got run over and the driver just dragged it off the road and left it under some bushes by the gates. It wasn't found till next morning. It was as near dead as makes no difference, back broken — and practically every other bone as well. I don't know whether it had suffered or not, lying out all night, it was probably unconscious. But Foster was heartbroken. He wouldn't talk about it, never mentioned it again, but he cried like one of the little kids — he'd be thirteen or fourteen at the time.'

A nurse put her head round the door and gave Lambert an enquiring look. 'I'm just off,' he told her. He got to his feet.

'Thanks for the chat,' Dalby said. 'Helped to break the monotony.'

Lambert felt a sharp pang of hunger as he walked back to the exit. There was a snack bar opposite the hospital and he went inside.

He stood at the counter with his ham roll and cup of coffee. Surely it was at Lineholt that Foster had bought some old factory months ago? He cast his mind back to the conversation he'd had in the pub with Rossiter, the young executive from Foster's solicitors. Yes, an old plating works, Rossiter had said, over at Lineholt.

He asked the proprietor if he knew of any such place that had changed hands earlier in the year.

'The Crusader works,' the man said at once. 'My nephew works there. It changed hands back in the spring. It's picked up no end since then, the new management's made all the difference.' He mentioned the location, on the southern edge of Lineholt. 'They're taking on extra labour now, don't see much of that round here these days.'

Lambert made a detour and found the works without difficulty. He got out of his car and went inside the gates, strolled about for a minute or two. The entrance and forecourt were clean and tidy. The exterior of the buildings had been smartened up; the gates, the notice board, the woodwork, were all freshly painted.

A little knot of men in overalls came out of a side door and dispersed in different directions. No idle chatter, Lambert noted, no standing about with hands in pockets and heads thrown back in loud laughter. A woman came down the front steps and walked across to an annexe with the same air of purpose and controlled haste.

Lambert walked thoughtfully back to his car. Vera Foster was dead against her husband buying the Lineholt works, Rossiter had said, but Foster managed to talk her round in the end. Was that piece of opposition one straw too many for Foster? Did he feel he'd had enough of Vera's irrational obstinacy, she'd have to go? Did he begin to prepare a plan, working out the details, ready for the moment when all the pieces would fall into place? Foster didn't mind waiting, Dalby had said, grinning at him from his bandages and plasters in the infirmary.

*

He was clearing his desk at the end of the day when he remembered he'd still done nothing about the business Edith Jordan had spoken of buying. He sat for some time pondering what to do about it.

It was likely that Miss Jordan was using the services of one or more of the Cannonbridge estate agents to locate a suitable business. But he couldn't just walk into each agency in turn and ask if she was on their books, what her instructions had been. No matter how he stressed the need to keep the matter confidential, not a word to be mentioned to Miss Jordan, he well knew that the next time she showed her face inside the doors, someone would give her a detailed run-down of his visit.

And there was the matter of fairness to Miss Jordan herself. She was, after all, not only not proven guilty of any wrongdoing, she was not even under serious suspicion of any crime. An estate agent would hesitate to go forward in a transaction with someone who had just been the subject of police enquiries, particularly an enquiry concerning the prospective purchase of property.

He walked over to the window and stood looking down at the forecourt. Better scrub the idea of a visit to the offices. The enquiries must be made by phone. And they must not appear to be enquiries but calls from Miss Jordan herself, to ask what progress the agents were making on her behalf.

He pressed his forehead against the pane. He couldn't make the calls himself, his voice sounded as if it issued from a spot just above his boots, he rated its chances of being accepted as a woman's voice at about one in two hundred thousand. He'd have to get some female to make the calls.

Another minute or two of the pressure of cold glass threw up in Lambert's brain the name of Woman Police Constable Maggie Purslow. Maggie was an athletic and muscular young woman, energetic and keen. She had recently begun to cherish ambitions towards detective work—and she was an enthusiastic member of a local amateur dramatic group.

'She'll do!' Lambert said aloud. He went off at once in search of her but she'd already gone off duty. He left word that she was to contact him next morning.

And bright and early next day—in fact one and a quarter minutes after receiving his message—Maggie presented herself in Lambert's office.

Her face was flushed and she was out of breath from having hurled herself up the stairs and along the corridors at breakneck speed, but she still looked reasonably trim and well groomed, as she usually managed to do at the start of the day. Her long thick hair—the colour of the hide of an old donkey—was neatly skewered on top of her head, a position it often succeeded in maintaining for as long as an hour or two.

Lambert offered Maggie no explanation as to what he was up to, he merely outlined what he wanted her to do.

He told her that Miss Jordan's voice probably wasn't well known to any of the clerks in the various offices. And Miss Jordan didn't seem the type to inject chatty remarks of a personal nature into business conversations. All Maggie had to do was keep strictly to the point and the risk of her being detected was slight.

There was no doubt about her response. 'Just give me the chance!' she said, with intense interest apparent in every line of her long and somewhat irregular features. Lambert gave her a demonstration of Edith Jordan's clipped tones and Maggie mimicked them till he was satisfied she could produce a passable imitation.

She could hardly be persuaded to wait till later in the morning before putting her dramatic skills to the test. 'You can't go phoning the agents too early,' Lambert said. Calls made during the busy part of the day would be far less likely to be remembered clearly afterwards, possibly referred to in conversation with Miss Jordan herself when next she had dealings with the agents.

'Edith Jordan was the temporary nurse out at Lynwood when Vera Foster committed suicide,' Maggie said. She tilted back her head and gave the sergeant a look of deep curiosity. 'Going to tell me what all this is about?'

Lambert looked back at her without speaking. He had already stressed the need for great discretion — in the police station as well as outside it.

'No, you're not going to tell me,' Maggie answered herself. She ran a hand over her mutinous hair while she studied him for a moment or two longer.

'My sister,' she said in an idle tone that was in contrast to the alert look in her pale grey eyes, 'worked for three weeks last summer as a temporary secretary for Mr Gerald Foster, in the Cannonbridge Thrift Society.' Lambert received this information in silence.

'My sister's a student,' Maggie went on. 'She does office work in the vacations, she's on the books of the Cannon-bridge Staff Agency. They sent her to the Thrift Society while Foster's secretary was on holiday.' Still Lambert said nothing.

'She's a very pretty girl.' Maggie gestured an outline. 'Exceptionally well endowed. She has a high old time on some of her jobs. Often with the bosses.' She gave Lambert a level look. 'Might be interesting to know how she got on with Gerald Foster.'

'It might indeed,' Lambert said in an equally idle tone. 'You'll be seeing her soon?'

She shook her head; a hairclip slipped down her cheek and hung suspended from a strand of hair. 'Not till Christmas.' She retrieved the clip and stabbed it back on to her scalp. 'But she often rings up to talk to Mum.'

'Have a word with her next time she rings,' Lambert said. 'Casually, mind.' He stood up. 'You can start phon-ing the estate agents around eleven.'

He wasn't present at her performance — she had no wish for an audience. His instructions were precise: Find out the date on which Edith Jordan first put her name on the books of any of the agents, the top price she was prepared to pay for a business, and how she intended to finance the purchase.

With her first two calls Maggie had little luck. All she discovered was that Miss Jordan was on the books of both firms. But the calls gave her confidence; both times she was unquestioningly accepted as Miss Jordan.

She dialled the third number more boldly. 'This is Miss Jordan,' she told the clerk in a crisp, positive tone. 'Edith Jordan, Orchard House School.'

'Oh yes, Miss Jordan,' the girl said at once. 'I'll get your file.' She came back a few moments later. 'I'm afraid nothing's come in since you last spoke to us, nothing really suitable.'

'It's been quite some time now.' Maggie allowed a trace of irritation to creep into her voice. 'It must be, what?'

'February 8th,' the girl said. 'That's what we've got down here. But of course you didn't give us definite instructions then, if you remember, you were just making preliminary enquiries, finding out price levels and so on. September 18th, that was when you gave definite instructions, so it isn't really all that long.'

'I suppose not,' Maggie said. 'Would it help at all if I was prepared to go a little higher on the price? Not that I want to raise the figure if I can help it.'

'No, of course not. Not when it's your own capital you're using.'

'My top limit, the one I originally—'

'Twenty-five thousand — that ought to be enough for the type of property you want. I don't really think raising the figure would help, it isn't the price that's the trouble, you see, it's the fact that you're so specific—'

'Yes, I do see that. And of course increasing the figure

could be a bit tricky for me.'

'Yes, it's not as if you were going through a bank or building society where you might be able to persuade them to lend you a little more. You've got to be careful when you're financing it entirely yourself. We never like clients to over-commit themselves, it simply doesn't pay.'

'I must just be patient then,' Maggie said on a farewell note.

'Don't worry,' the girl said cheerfully. 'We'll find the right business for you one of these days. Probably a lot sooner than you think.'

Maggie rushed off at once in search of Sergeant Lambert. She found him striding along one of the ground-floor corridors. As soon as he caught sight of her flashing smile he knew she'd been successful. He stood listening to her with his head bent.

'September 18th,' he said reflectively when she'd finished. Edith Jordan had given definite instructions to the agents while she was at Lynwood. Three days before Vera Foster died.

Towards noon next day Lambert had his call from London, giving details of the wills of Edith Jordan's mother and Mrs Lydiatt. When the call was over he sat back and looked at the notes he'd made.

Mrs Jordan had left everything to her only child, Edith Margaret, the total estate amounting to just under two thousand pounds. Mrs Jordan hadn't owned the house she had lived in with her daughter; they were tenants.

Mrs Lydiatt's property was a good deal more sizable. Her entire estate, which included the house and land at Fairhaven, some rented dwellings in Mildenhall, lease-hold business property in Cannonbridge, a considerable holding of stocks and shares, came to very nearly a quarter of a million pounds.

Her will was dated eight years ago. There were bequests to various charities, religious organizations, former servants and so on. The residue went to cousins in Australia. A legacy to Miss Edith Margaret Jordan was for a sum of six thousand pounds.

CHAPTER 10

Lambert stared down at his notes. So on the death of her mother, Edith Jordan not only didn't own a roof over her head, she had very possibly been given notice to quit the house she had grown up in.

With less than two thousand pounds behind her she was in no position to buy a house for herself. Residential employment would seem to be the only solution for a woman in her position.

At that time she must have been in her early thirties. When the doctor suggested the post at Mrs Lydiatt's Edith must have felt relief, to say the least.

At first she might have looked on the Fairhaven post as a temporary fill-in, till she could decide how to spend the rest of her life. But time would pass and she would settle into the comfortable life in Hawthorn Lane. And it seemed she got on well with Mrs Lydiatt.

If she left, where was she to go? To some other similar post, possibly less agreeable?

It was easy to guess at what might have happened. Miss Jordan perhaps showing signs of restlessness, speaking to Mrs Lydiatt of the future, the need to provide for herself on some secure basis, possibly mentioning her wish one day to own a small business.

And Mrs Lydiatt, understanding and reassuring, smiling, saying: Stay with me, my dear, we suit each other very well. You see me out and I'll look after you. I'll leave you enough to start your business.

Eight years ago six thousand pounds was not an ungenerous sum; it would certainly have bought a small run-down business.

But the world had changed gear since then, values were very different now. Mrs Lydiatt would probably have been astounded to learn how her estate had been valued at her death.

She was over eighty when she died. In all likelihood she had ceased to keep up with what was happening in the world beyond Hawthorn Lane. It probably never occurred to her to update the amounts of her bequests in the light of inflation.

And Edith Jordan would have believed herself provided for. After signing the will Mrs Lydiatt would probably have told Edith she had no need to worry any more, it was all arranged. Very unlikely that Mrs Lydiatt would mention the actual figure, a woman of that generation, brought up to consider discussion of such matters ill-bred.

And Edith would trust her, would believe the sum to be enough, probably on the generous side. She may even have had visions of being left a small fortune, seeing that Mrs Lydiatt had no close relatives.

And then when she learned the contents of the will after Mrs Lydiatt's death, Edith must have had a tremendous shock. The legacy wasn't enough to buy the most miserable of properties, let alone a business of potential in a good locality.

Lambert pressed his fingers into his forehead. It all squared with what the newsagent had told him in the shop in Hawthorn Lane. On a day not long after Mrs Lydiatt's funeral, the day the account of her funeral was carried in the local paper, Miss Jordan had said she must look for another residential post. She would know the size of her legacy at that time and she made no mention of looking for a business.

That date, Lambert reflected, would be some time in January. Mrs Lydiatt died on January 3rd, so the account of her funeral would probably be published somewhere between January 10th and 17th.

And yet, only two or three weeks later, on February 8th, Edith Jordan was writing a letter to the Cannon-bridge Staff Agency in which she made mention of buying a business. And her preliminary enquiries to the estate agents had also been made on February 8th.

So at some time betweeen the middle of January and February 8th something happened which caused Miss Jordan to believe that not only could she now afford to start looking for a business but she could finance the purchase herself when the time came. And she had mentioned a sum of twenty-five thousand pounds.

All the capital she could have was whatever she had made by way of investment from the couple of thousand her mother had left her, together with what she had managed to save from her salary at Fairhaven and the legacy of six thousand from Mrs Lydiatt. Nowhere near twenty-five thousand pounds.

He frowned down at the desk. Suppose the event that had changed Edith Jordan's mind was indeed, as Kelsey suggested, that Foster had learned of the building site and gone over to Mildenhall, met Miss Jordan and talked to her, been struck by the possibility that here might be the ally he was seeking.

Had Foster then gone away and thought about her, later returned and begun to make tentative suggestions, discovered they were falling on fertile soil, and after further conversations entered into an arrangement whereby he would end up a widower and Edith would end up the owner of the business she'd always wanted?

If so, then the agreement must have been settled by February 8th for on that date Miss Jordan was ringing estate agents and writing to Miss Unwin, confident she was now in a position to start realizing her dream.

And the moment Foster entered into such an arrangement there would be an abrupt end to his interest in the building plot — for he must do nothing which could later on reveal that there had been any association between himself and Miss Jordan before she set foot in Lynwood.

So Foster, ever the man of business, constitutionally unable to see a good site go to some total stranger, picks up the phone and passes the word on to Ormrod.

What I've got to do now, Lambert thought, is discover the date on which Foster rang Ormrod about the site. If that date was very close either way to February 8th, then it might indeed begin to look as if Kelsey's notions weren't moonshine after all.

Now, how to discover that date? He couldn't go back to Ormrod and ask more questions. Ormrod's curiosity, already beginning to stir at the end of their conversation a couple of days ago, would certainly be roused.

He'd be sure to tell Foster the police were showing an interest in the date, in the purchase of the Fairhaven plot, and that would most certainly give Foster cause for thought, whether he was innocent or guilty. And in either eventuality that was the last thing Lambert wanted.

Ah — the estate agent! Ormrod had rung the agent as soon as he heard about the Fairhaven site. All Lambert had to do now was find out the date on which he'd phoned the agent.

He grinned. Another little job for Maggie Purslow. And while she was at it she could find out the date on which the Mildenhall Gazette had carried the account of Mrs Lydiatt's funeral. Not that the exact date seemed all that important but Lambert could hear the echo of the Chief's signature tune: When you think you've found out, check it. And then check it again.

He cleared away his papers and went off in search of Maggie Purslow.

*

It took Maggie very little time next morning to deal with the matter. By ten o'clock she'd discovered that a girl she'd been at school with worked for the agents who'd handled the Fairhaven business. A girl who'd played net-ball when Maggie was team captain, a girl who could keep her mouth shut — and not ask awkward questions. At five minutes past ten Maggie went into action.

At lunchtime she went briskly down to the canteen. Her hair had already won the first round of its ceaseless battle against the pins, and a couple of large tresses had leapt from restraint.

She spotted Sergeant Lambert alone at a corner table, crouching over his braised liver and carrots with a brooding expression. She strode across and pulled back a chair.

Lambert glanced up at her with a preoccupied look. She dropped on the table in front of him a copy of the Mildenhall Gazette. 'Page 6,' she said. 'Mrs Lydiatt's funeral. January 12th.'

Lambert's face cleared. He laid down his knife and fork. Maggie flung herself into the chair.

'Ormrod phoned the estate agent on February 8th, the agent took him over to see the plot on the morning of the 9th. Ormrod decided to buy the plot on the 10th. His offer was accepted in writing on February 15th.' She laid a slip of paper on the table. 'It's all down there.'

Lambert half rose from his seat. He leaned across and took her face in both hands, he planted a kiss on her cheek. 'Oh, Maggie Purslow,' he said with fervour, 'if ever you should think of getting married, I'll put a pound note towards your present.'

'I'll not get married,' she said. 'Mug's game.'

He lifted the stray locks of hair up on top of her head and tucked them into the main structure, achieving a rather striking Japanese effect. He patted her cheek.

'Then let me know when it's your birthday. I have the very thing for you. A full half-pound packet of cloves.'

Later that same evening Chief Inspector Kelsey returned to Cannonbridge and in the course of the following morning managed a word with Sergeant Lambert. But it was no more than a word; the Chief was up to his eyes in it.

'Four o'clock,' he said to Lambert. 'My office. Come hell or high water.'

Lambert took along with him the little additional file he was building up on the Foster case. Kelsey listened to Lambert's account of his doings, he read over the sequence of events as Lambert had listed them . . . Mrs Lydiatt dies, Mrs Lydiatt is buried, and so on, with dates and places. He nodded from time to time, grunted, asked an occasional question.

When he had finished he looked up at Lambert with approval. 'Very interesting,' he said. 'On September 7th Edith Jordan arrives at Lynwood. On September 18th she's able to give the agents specific instructions about the business, she now definitely knows she can raise twenty-five thousand pounds.'

He linked his hands behind his head. 'We could always seek Miss Jordan out and ask her: What money are you going to use to buy your business? What happened in September to put you in such a firm position that you could actually instruct the agents?' His green eyes shone. 'Either she can tell us or she can't.'

He saw Lambert's look. 'Don't worry,' he said with a grin, 'we're not going to ask those questions just yet. We've a few other things to find out first. All we've really got at this stage is the faintest possible hint of a link between Foster and Edith via the building plot.'

He listened with frowning concentration to what Lambert told him about his visit to Lineholt, his chats with Weaver and Dalby.

'Foster had a strange childhood,' Kelsey said. 'Bound to have been some emotional crippling.' Foster might well not have the normal range of emotions, might have been able to look on Vera as a wasting business asset to be disposed of at the right moment.

'And he wasn't there when Vera died,' he said. 'If he could arrange for it to happen painlessly behind his back he might be able to think of it as not a crime at all, just some kind of impersonal disposal.'

He rubbed his chin. 'He helped to save her life before, he might feel he'd given her nine years more of life than she'd wanted. He could say: What has she got to look forward to? She dreads growing old, she's unable to make friends. Folk are very good at believing what they want to believe. He might even come to believe that she did actually take her own life.'

He stared down at the floor. 'And Edith Jordan, her emotional development doesn't seem to have been normal either.' A close and restricted life, ingrown, narrow, little opportunity for marriage, surroundings classically guaranteed to induce the growth of deep and eccentric emotions.

'She was probably feeling savage resentment over the size of her legacy from Mrs Lydiatt when Foster popped up and started making his suggestions. He offers her a substantial sum to set her up in the business she's always wanted. She sees his offer as her last chance of independence. If she takes another resident post she'll never again have confidence in what she's told about provision being made for her.'

'She certainly wouldn't enjoy the prospect of a penny-pinching old age,' Lambert said. She'd grown used to a good standard of living. And behind her she had a history of having her life gobbled up by invalid women, she might feel that in striking at Vera she was striking at those other two gobbling women.

She might well sympathize with Foster's feeling that his wife was an incubus, might feel that the money he proposed to hand over would be some sort of recompense for her own wasted life, that Vera must pay for what the other two women had done to her.

'And what Foster suggests is in no way horrifying,' Kelsey said. 'She isn't called on physically to strike or wound, to strangle or smother. She isn't even asked to sit and watch Vera die. All she has to do is increase a dose to a lethal amount, return to Vera's bedroom after a sufficient lapse of time and arrange things to look like suicide.'

'That could have taken a bit of doing,' Lambert said. Propping up the body, getting the postcard from the desk drawer, putting the photograph of Duncan Murdoch under Vera's fingers, switching on the radio, dealing with the keys, the lights.

Kelsey shrugged. 'I dare say she was able to face five or ten minutes' unpleasant duties in return for what — fifteen, twenty, twenty-five thousand pounds, whatever Foster promised her. After it was all over and she got back to her own room she probably took a good strong sleeping draught.' When Alma Driscoll knocked on her door next morning Edith was still sound asleep, difficult to rouse.

'It wasn't as if she was being asked to kill a woman she knew,' he said. 'She'd never set eyes on Mrs Foster before she went to Lynwood.'

Lambert moved his head as if to say, Yes, I grant you it all sounds possible. Edith would know when she entered the house what she was to do, she wouldn't permit herself to grow in any way attached to the victim, would consider her as a warder might look on a prisoner sentenced to death or a nurse look on a patient with a terminal illness.

She would give what care and attention were necessary but blank off all emotion, so that the end when it came would have as little effect on herself as possible, certainly wouldn't lead to sleepless nights or a troubled conscience.

Lambert suddenly saw why Edith might have taken the post at Orchard House School after the funeral, the attractions of a place full of young girls, no sick women to be nursed, no old women to be waited on, nothing to remind her of the past, a relief, a pause, a breathing-space, perhaps even a sense of being a girl again herself, at the beginning of a hopeful life full of possibilities.

A thought struck him. 'Blackmail—if they did make such an arrangement, mightn't Foster be laying himself open to blackmail later on? Mightn't Edith come back for more money? And keep coming back?'

Kelsey made a dismissive gesture. 'Edith knows—and Foster's well aware she knows—that he's prepared to kill if people get in his way. And what threat could she make? Tell all? She'd incriminate herself as much as him. And the reverse—the possibility of Foster blackmailing Edith—that would be a totally pointless operation.'

He expelled a long breath. 'Now—opportunity and method.'

'Not much doubt about opportunity,' Lambert said.

Kelsey stared up at the ceiling. 'As to method, fake suicide would strike Foster as the most obvious course. Vera had already attempted suicide, she left no note then, she need leave no note this time, so there wouldn't be that difficulty to overcome.'

'How do we know she left no note before?' Lambert asked suddenly.

Kelsey sat up and looked at the sergeant for several seconds. 'That's right,' he said at last. 'How do we know?' They were both silent. 'We've only Foster's word that she didn't leave a note.'

CHAPTER 11

The Chief cast his mind back to what Foster had told them about that earlier attempt at suicide.

Duncan Murdoch's funeral had taken place in the morning. Vera went through it with composure. When it was all over she told Hetty Attwood, the Lynwood housekeeper at that time, that she was going up to her room to rest. Foster was in the study office on the ground floor, dealing with urgent business matters that had arisen since Murdoch's death.

A little later Hetty went softly upstairs to see if Vera was all right, if she wanted anything. She found the bedroom door locked. She became alarmed and tried to rouse Vera by knocking and calling. When this failed she ran down to the study to summon Foster. He broke down the bedroom door.

Vera had taken a large dose of her father's sleeping pills. Foster phoned for Doctor Tredgold while Hetty tried to revive her mistress.

'Foster definitely told me there was no letter,' Kelsey said. 'I remember very clearly.'

'If there was a letter,' Lambert said, 'Foster could have suggested to Hetty that they should destroy it to make it look like an accidental overdose. Hetty would go along with that.'

Kelsey wrinkled his brow. 'We know without doubt that there was no letter when Vera died.' That was sworn to at the inquest by Alma Driscoll and the two Pritchard men as well as by Edith Jordan. 'So we would expect to find no letter at the first attempt.' Would-be suicides normally followed a similar pattern at every attempt. 'Now Foster says there was no letter the first time. But suppose Foster is lying and there was a letter, then Vera's behaviour was different on the two occasions. That would suggest that only one of the two attempts was genuine. We know the first attempt was genuine so the second was faked.'

Lambert frowned. 'You're saying that if there was a letter the first time then Vera's death looks like murder.'

'That's it.'

Lambert sat frowning in thought. Anyone trying to fake a suicide would always have to face this problem of the farewell communication. Very difficult to forge a convincing suicide letter. A better alternative would surely be to dispense with any form of note or letter, do what one could with such props as were available . . . as, for instance, an old picture postcard from the victim's dear departed father . . .

'That business of the postcard,' he said, 'the underlined words. She could have left something like that the first time, some kind of indirect statement that Foster and Hetty Attwood removed or destroyed.'

'She could indeed,' Kelsey said. 'We've got to find out beyond doubt exactly what Vera did that first time.' He screwed up his face. 'That means getting in touch with Hetty, she's the only one who can tell us for sure.'

Hetty had left Lynwood back in the spring, Kelsey didn't know where she was now. 'Alma Driscoll might know her address,' he said. But they couldn't go marching into Lynwood to question Alma.

'It certainly seems very convenient for Foster,' he said, 'that Hetty left Lynwood in the spring. He'd been trying to get rid of her for years. Then all at once she suddenly decides to oblige him and take herself off, just at a time when it will allow him to introduce Edith Jordan into the household a little later on.'

'Hetty had reached retiring age,' Lambert pointed out.

'My impression is that she'd reached retiring age quite some time before, and that she managed to resist all suggestions of retirement.' Kelsey narrowed his eyes. 'The most obvious time for Foster to carry out the murder was during one of Vera's attacks of sciatica. Hetty normally took care of Vera during those attacks, so first Foster must get rid of Hetty. How very cooperative of Hetty all at once to decide the time had finally come to pack her bags.'

'But perhaps that's what did happen,' Lambert said. 'Simply that she finally decided she was too old to go on working. Or maybe Foster stepped up his offer of financial provision, made it too attractive to turn down.'

'Of course we could be confusing cause and effect,' Kelsey said. 'It could have been the other way round, Hetty decided to retire and that gave Foster the idea of introducing an outsider into the household next time Vera had one of her attacks. That could have been what started his whole train of thought about the method of murder.'

Lambert moved his shoulders, said nothing.

'Anyway,' Kelsey said, 'whatever the reason and whatever way round it was, Hetty did leave Lynwood.' He tapped the desk. 'Foster instructs Miss Jordan to put herself on the books of the agency his wife normally uses. She's to ask for the kind of post which will in due course crop up at Lynwood. She's to make sure she takes only short-term jobs so she'll be available when the time comes.'

He frowned. 'You notice that as soon as the Lynwood episode is over, Miss Jordan suddenly changes her tune as far as the agency is concerned. She's no longer so set on very short postings, all at once she's perfectly happy to stay on at Orchard House for the best part of a term, just because she's taken a fancy to the place.'

He sat back. 'She told Miss Unwin she wanted short postings so she could be free to look at properties, not to be tied down if a suitable property suddenly turned up. That reason still exists—but the real reason no longer exists, Vera Foster is now dead and buried.'

He passed a hand across his jaw. 'So we come to the murder itself. It must take place when Edith Jordan is alone in the house at night with Mrs Foster, so it must be on a Thursday night when Alma Driscoll can be relied on not to return before morning. Foster removes himself on business. Edith gives Vera her bedtime drink of chocolate laced with a fatal dose of her pain-killers.'

'Edith said she gave Vera one tablet with the chocolate at a quarter to ten,' Lambert pointed out. 'We assumed that Vera took the fatal dose herself shortly afterwards with a drink of water. Now you're saying she was given the whole dose in one go.'

'I can't see that it matters,' Kelsey said. 'Nothing there that quarrels with the medical evidence.' All that evidence could say was that the fatal dose had been taken at some time between half past nine and half past ten.

'Another thing,' Lambert said. 'Doctor Tredgold prescribed another bottle of tablets that very day. Vera had almost finished the last bottle. Wasn't that running it a bit fine as far as Foster was concerned? He couldn't be certain Vera would ask to see the doctor that morning, he couldn't be certain she'd ask him for another bottle of tablets, or that he would prescribe them if she did ask.'

'Tredgold said Vera had been taking a fair number of tablets, more than he liked.' Kelsey stretched out his arms and flexed the muscles. 'She probably hadn't been taking as many as he believed. Foster could have been steadily filching them without her noticing. He probably had a nice little store of tablets stacked away; I doubt if he needed to rely on Tredgold prescribing a new bottle.'

'And the business of the keys,' Lambert said. 'She'd have to lock the door leading to Foster's bedroom, put the keys of both doors on the dressing-chest and then leave Mrs Foster's room, locking the door behind her with a third key. But no one admitted knowing of any spare key to either of the two doors.'

Kelsey gave a dismissing wave of his hand. 'That doesn't mean Foster didn't have one.' He leaned back in his chair. 'It all fits. Where we actually know a fact, it fits.' He fixed Lambert with a glittering eye. 'I defy you to mention one single fact that we actually know for a fact, that doesn't square with all I've said.' Lambert said nothing. 'There you are, then,' Kelsey said with satisfaction.

He whistled through his teeth. 'Foster made one stupid mistake. He should have let the building site go. He should have turned his back on it, let some stranger buy it and develop it, take the profit. But he couldn't do it, his nature was too strong for him. He had to pass the word on to someone he knew.' He grinned. 'He'd have been a better murderer if he was a worse businessman.'

'We can't prove any of it,' Lambert reminded him. 'You're talking as if Foster's going to be arrested and charged. It looks to me as if he has every chance of getting away with it.' He gave the Chief a level look. 'That is, if he actually did it.' Constructing a nice neat theory might be a very satisfying exercise, it didn't necessarily have any connection with the hard reality of what actually happened.

Kelsey ignored the observation. 'We're a long way from the end of the road yet,' he said briskly. He stroked his nose. 'Alma Driscoll. The Fox and Hounds. Thursday evening.' My friend Rosie Trewin and I, Alma had said, we usually drop in at the pub for an hour or two. 'Buy her a drink,' he said. 'Chat her up.' Kelsey wouldn't have objected to that part of the job himself, wouldn't at all have minded slipping an arm round Alma's curvy waist.

'Right,' Lambert said without enthusiasm. In his eyes Alma was too old, too fat and too vulgar to be of any personal interest.

'Find out where Hetty Attwood lives these days,' Kelsey

said. 'And anything else you can get out of Alma.'

'I take it,' Lambert said, 'we can forget about Foster having his eye on Alma?'

'I can't think there's anything in that.' Kelsey had pondered the possibility once or twice but he simply couldn't see the two of them together. 'I doubt if Alma will be working for Foster much longer. He'll probably put Lynwood on the market. A place that size, he must be rattling round in it on his own, I shouldn't think it was ever really his style.' And he would surely like to be rid of memories of Vera.

Kelsey could see him in a bachelor service flat, no frills, no worries, a restaurant if he was hungry, his mind free to deal with what really absorbed him; business. 'My guess is Alma will soon be looking for another job. I doubt if Foster will spend much time thinking about her.'

CHAPTER 12

At twenty minutes to eight on Thursday evening Lambert duly seated himself in a corner of the saloon bar at the Fox and Hounds and hid behind an evening paper to avoid unwanted friendly recognition. He glanced discreetly out at each fresh arrival. Rosie and I usually go along to the pub about eight, Alma had told Kelsey, we stay an hour or two, then I catch the half past ten bus back to Abberley.

Lambert was reduced to reading the classified ads before the swing doors opened and Alma entered with another woman, equally plump and cheerful-looking, with bottle-blonde hair built up to an elaborate structure on top of her head.

Lambert lowered his paper, picked up his glass and drained the last mouthful. Alma glanced energetically about and at once recognized the sergeant.

'Hello, there!' she called with a friendly smile, delighted at the sight of a good-looking unattached male apparently at a loose end; Alma's notion of the ideal vision to greet her gaze at the start of an evening.

Lambert walked casually across to the bar and set down his empty glass. He looked across at the two women with amiable invitation. Alma needed no further encouragement, she came over at once with the blonde close behind.

'I don't believe you've met my friend Rosie Trewin,' she said.

'I've heard all about you from Alma,' Rosie said with a wink and a smile.

'What'll it be, then?' Lambert asked with false cheer.

'Lager and lime for Rosie,' Alma said with well-practised swiftness. 'Vodka and lime for me. It's ever so nice bumping into you like this.'

Lambert had a horrid vision of being stuck with the pair of them till closing time, unable to prise Alma loose from Rosie, paying for their drinks and learning nothing of any value, but to his relief he saw a glance pass between the two women. A glance which clearly said on Alma's side: With any luck this is me fixed up for the evening, I'm bagging this one; and on Rosie's side: That's OK by me, I've spotted one or two other likely lads.

Lambert carried the drinks over to his corner table and they all three sat down. Alma leaned well back into her seat but Rosie remained upright on the edge of the red velvet banquette, ready to take off as soon as civility allowed.

It didn't take her long to finish her drink. 'No thanks, don't you bother about me,' she said with breezy firmness when Lambert offered to buy her another. 'I'm just off to powder my nose.' She gathered up her handbag. 'I see one or two friends along the bar, I'll probably have a word with them afterwards.' She gave Alma a half-wink, smiled at Lambert. 'Enjoy yourselves.'

'She's a good sort,' Alma said as Rosie vanished through a curtained doorway. 'She used to work at the village pub before she was married. I often used to pop along and have a rattle with her in the afternoons.' In a couple of minutes Lambert had steered the conversation round to domestic service and thence to Lynwood.

'How's Mr Foster settling down?' he was able to ask after another minute or two.

She pulled down the corners of her mouth. 'He never was one to say much. Now he hardly says anything at all. Not that I see much of him. He's down at his office in the town all the time, he stays down there a lot later these days. Not that I blame him, it can't be very cheerful coming back home, being reminded all the time.'

She stared into her glass. 'He said something the other day about selling Lynwood.' She looked up at Lambert. 'Best thing you could do, I told him straight, clear out, make a fresh start. He's not all that old, he's younger than he looks.'

'Would you call him good-looking?' Lambert asked casually.

She shrugged. 'I never thought about it, I never noticed his looks. That type — the sort that lives for business — you never really think of them as men.' She gave the sergeant a bold, appraising, inviting look. 'Not my idea of a man, anyway. I just look on him as the boss, the man who pays my wages.' She looked down again at her glass. 'But you certainly couldn't call him ugly.'

'Perhaps he'll marry again one day.'

'I certainly hope so,' she said with force. 'He wants to find himself some nice homely woman, raise a family. It'd do him the world of good.' She looked up at Lambert. 'He never had a proper family life, not in his own childhood.'

'Did you know the family?'

She laughed. 'How old do you take me for? It was Hetty told me about them. Hetty Attwood, she used to work at Lynwood. She knew his parents years ago.' In another minute or two she was chatting about Hetty.

'She got ever so difficult in the last year or two before she left,' she said in a confidential tone. 'Mr Foster would have sacked her more than once, that I do know. But poor dear Mrs Foster, she wouldn't have it. Hetty had been her Dad's servant, you see.'

'Hetty wasn't sacked then, in the end?' Lambert asked. 'She just retired?'

Alma shrugged. 'She had to go, there couldn't be any argument about it. She was well turned sixty so they called it retirement, they didn't want any trouble.'

She leaned forward. 'She'd been nicking bits of stuff for years, we all knew about it, no one made any fuss, it was never anything you could call valuable. I reckon they looked on it as part of her perks. But one day she went too far, she pinched a brooch of Mrs Foster's, quite valuable.'

'How did she expect to get away with that?'

'I suppose she thought it wouldn't be missed. Mrs Foster hardly ever wore it. It belonged to her mother, it was very old-fashioned. Mrs Foster kept it in a velvet case at the back of a drawer in her bureau. One day Mr Foster showed her a picture of some jewellery in a magazine and he said, 'Isn't that brooch rather like that one of your mother's? It's a shame not to wear it, that style's coming back again and it's very fine workmanship.' So Mrs Foster went to look for the brooch, to compare it.

'But she couldn't find it and there was a great hullabaloo. Of course we all knew who'd pinched it, we all knew Hetty's little ways. Mr Foster said to his wife, "We don't want to call in the police. Your father wouldn't have liked that. We'll settle it ourselves."'

'There wasn't any question of it being an outside job, he said, it had to be someone in the house. He said he was going to search through Hetty's things—and mine too, of course. He couldn't just do Hetty's, that wouldn't look right.

'Mrs Foster didn't like it but she could see it would have to be done. Mr Foster went through my things first and of course there was nothing there. Then he went through Hetty's, with Hetty standing there in the room, denying it all as bold as brass.

'And sure enough there the brooch was, hidden inside a rolled-up pair of stockings. There were some other things too that she'd nicked but he didn't bother about those, they were just a load of old junk, stuff that had been more of less thrown out. She was like a magpie, she liked anything bright and glittery.'

She looked reflectively at Lambert. 'Of course, she had to go. Even Mrs Foster could see that.'

'Did Hetty make a fuss about going?'

'Not really. There wasn't much she could say. Mrs Foster was very upset but all the same I could see she was relieved Hetty was going at last.'

'Where did she go?'

Alma bit her lip. 'I've got it written down somewhere. Not that I've ever needed the address. Hetty's never had any letters come for her, or anything like that.'

'Didn't she have any friends? Surely she lived a long time in Abberley?'

'I don't know of any friends. She wasn't one to make friends. She kept very much to herself. Very old-fashioned she was too, very narrow in her ways.'

'How did you get on with her?'

She pulled a face. 'When I first went to Lynwood Hetty thought I'd come to steal her job, but when she realized she was going to be kept on as well then she did improve a bit towards me. Not that we were ever bosom friends, but I made it my business to get on with her.'

She spread her hands. 'I don't like a nasty atmosphere

in a house. I like things nice and friendly. But I could never really like Hetty. I was sorry for her in some ways. She'd been a good worker in her time, a good cook too. But she'd got a bit odd and her work wasn't up to much any more. In my opinion she took barefaced advantage of Mrs Foster, her devotion to her father. And I know that was what Mr Foster thought, for I heard him say as much to Mrs Foster more than once. Hetty had got away with it so long she thought she could get away with anything. I really think she'd begun to fancy they'd let her soldier on at Lynwood till she died, drawing her wages and doing less and less for them.'

'Does Hetty know Mrs Foster's dead?' Lambert asked suddenly.

She gaped at him. She set down her glass. 'Do you know, I don't suppose she does. I can't think who'd have taken the trouble to write and tell her.'

'She might have read it in the paper.'

'She doesn't live round here. Not in this county. She wouldn't see the local papers.' She screwed up her face. 'Where was it she went? By the sea somewhere.'

She struck her forehead. 'Norfolk! That's it! I'm sure it was! It's a very short address. I remember thinking that when I wrote it down. She hardly spoke a word the day she was leaving. Marching about with her nose in the air like some duchess.'

'Norfolk,' Lambert said, twirling his glass.

'Some village by the sea. It's coming back to me!' she cried in triumph. 'Marshes, something to do with marshes. She was going to live with her sister. The sister's older than Hetty. She's a widow, she was married to a fisherman but he was drowned in those floods they had there twenty or thirty years ago. Hetty was going to live with her in this old cottage, she'd like that, being so old-fashioned herself.'

Lambert picked up her glass. 'Another of the same?'

She nodded, smiling. 'And something to eat?'

'I've just had supper at Rosie's. But I could manage a packet of crisps.'

As Lambert stood at the bar he glanced about and saw Rosie sitting in a corner with a powerfully built man who looked as if he'd been a boxer. He had his arm round her waist and she was screeching with laughter at something he'd said.

Alma was smoking a cigarette when he got back with the drinks. 'Can't give them up,' she said cheerfully. 'They'll kill me one day, I expect, but what the hell. A short life and a merry, that's what I say.' She stopped smiling abruptly and her face fell into melancholy lines. She looked all at once a different woman, older, more serious, a good deal sharper.

'Poor Mrs Foster,' she said with a loud sigh. 'You couldn't help liking her. There was something, I don't know—' She glanced away. 'Childish, I suppose, as if you felt you had to look after her.'

She smiled slightly. 'I was younger than her but I always felt a lot older. In ways of the world at any rate.' She sighed again. 'I've been over it all in my mind dozens of times, wondering if there was anything I could have said or done that would have made any difference.' She shook her head. 'I never come up with anything.'

She was silent for a moment, then she spoke in a lighter tone. 'When I first went to Lynwood, that wasn't all that long after Mr and Mrs Foster were married, I used to think how pretty she looked when she'd just had her hair done and she was wearing something soft and thin, like on a summer evening. That kind of thing always suited her.'

She shook her head. 'That type doesn't wear well, they get old quickly. That fine skin and pale colouring, they get to look washed out and haggard.' She put up a hand and patted her own shining, springing hair, abundant and warmly glowing, full of Titian lights under the wall-lamps.

She began to eat her crisps with an abstracted air. 'It gave me a horrible shock when I got back to Lynwood that morning and we found poor Mrs Foster.'

She drew a long quivering breath. 'Put me off porridge for the rest of my life. I just can't abide the smell of the stuff now, turns my stomach.' Lambert was mystified. 'Funny that.' She stared up at the ceiling. 'I liked it well enough before.'

'But you don't like it now,' Lambert said when it looked as if she wasn't going to explain.

'That I do not! When we found her, when Bob Pritchard broke down the door, I looked back along the corridor and there was old Ned Pritchard with Miss Jordan coming along behind him, and the smell of burning porridge floating up the stairs.'

She picked up a spent match from the ash-tray and began to grind a crisp into fragments. 'I didn't much notice it at the time. I was thinking about poor Mrs Foster and what we might find when we got inside the room.

'Bob got the door down and we all rushed in.' She threw down the match and picked up her glass, she took a long drink. She glanced over the top of the glass at Lambert and he saw the glitter of tears in her eyes. 'Afterwards, just the smell of porridge, it seemed to bring everything back to me. I said to Mr Foster, "You won't mind if I don't make porridge any more." He didn't ask me why not and I didn't tell him, not wanting to upset him. He just said, "Not in the least, you cook anything you like." He's not fussy about his food, he'd eat anything you put before him. I suppose that comes of being brought up in an orphanage.'

She set down her glass. 'Miss Jordan forgot to put the porridge in the Aga, though I did remind her last thing before I went off that afternoon.'

She moved her head. 'She made it right enough the time before, made it very nicely too. Not that she's ever done much cooking, needlework's more in her line.'

She opened her eyes wide at Lambert. 'She's wonderful with a needle. She has some beautiful blouses. And I saw her underwear when she was packing to leave. Pure silk, really lovely, fit for a duchess.'

She nibbled a crisp. 'When I came in I looked in the Aga to make sure the porridge was all right and it wasn't there. I thought, Oh well, Mrs Foster'll have to put up with rolled oats just this once, so I put the pan on to boil. Then I thought, I'll just pop upstairs with the tray of tea, it won't take a moment. But of course it was ages before I came down again and the porridge had boiled all over the stove.'

'Have another drink,' Lambert said.

'You can get me one in.' She grinned. 'But I'll have to go to the Ladies first or I'll burst.' She stood up. 'I'll have a word with Rosie, see how she's getting on.'

She glanced over to where Rosie was now lying back against the velvet upholstery. The superannuated boxer was kissing her on the cheek. 'She's getting on very well, if you ask me.' Alma went off through the curtained doorway.

If I don't get Hetty's address out of her here, Lambert thought glumly, I'll have to offer to run her back to Lynwood. He must get the address tonight, he couldn't play the same trick twice, drop into the pub again, it would be too glaringly obvious.

Alma came back through the curtain. On her way over to speak to Rosie she paused by Lambert's table.

'I've got it!' she said with triumph. 'It came to me all of a sudden in the whatsit.' She laughed. 'Hetty Attwood's address. I told you it was a short one. The Old Bakery, Longmarsh, Norfolk.'

*

It was after eleven when Lambert got back to his lodgings. His landlady had already gone to bed. He went into the kitchen to make himself some coffee. No fear of it keeping him awake. Head on the pillow and spark out, that was his style.

As he sat at the table, drinking the coffee and eating one of his landlady's excellent almond slices, he turned over in his mind Alma's story about the porridge.

It doesn't square with what I know of Edith Jordan, he thought. Efficient, attentive to detail—if she was asked to put the porridge in the oven overnight then she would certainly put it in, he'd be willing to bet money on that. She'd remembered two weeks before and Alma certainly expected her to remember again.

But she hadn't. A conscientious, well-organized, reliable woman, but she'd forgotten to cook the porridge . . . Or was it that she hadn't thought it necessary, knowing that Mrs Foster would never be able to eat it? Perhaps her nature had revolted against that macabre pretence, one last touch she found just a shade too repugnant, going through the pantomime of making porridge for a woman who would never again eat any kind of breakfast.

He picked up another almond slice and took a thoughtful bite. She could just have forgotten it, she could have been in such a tense, strung-up state that she took no conscious decision about it, all thought of it just went clean out of her head.

'Longmarsh,' Chief Inspector Kelsey said. He peered down at the map spread out on his desk. He ran a finger over the jagged outline of the Norfolk coast. 'We'll have a talk with Hetty Attwood.' He glanced briefly up at Sergeant Lambert. 'You'd better get on to Norwich. Find out if she's still living at the Old Bakery.' No point in driving all that way only to discover Hetty had gone off to the

Costa Brava on a pensioners' jaunt or had fallen down dead six months ago.

'Might just be able to fit it in the early part of next week.' Kelsey sucked on a tooth. 'Later in the week's no good. And the week after's impossible.' He straightened up and felt the muscles of his back speak in protest. Not as young as he used to be. He'd only just got around to accepting the notion, had strenuously resisted it in the face of increasing evidence.

He ran over the days in his mind. 'Monday, then,' he said. 'If at all possible.'

When Lambert left the Chief's office he went down to the canteen for a cup of coffee and a cheese sandwich. Over in a corner he saw Maggie Purslow sitting by herself; she was just about to begin an onslaught on a cup of tea and two very large and sticky doughnuts.

Lambert carried his tray across to her table and sat down. 'You'll get fat,' he told her.

Her long beaky nose dipped over the first succulent mouthful. 'I was going to come looking for you,' she said in a muffled tone. 'I spoke to my sister last night on the phone.' She leaned forward and a wisp of her donkey-brown hair trailed over the savaged doughnut. She flicked the hair aside and took another bite.

'She says forget the ladies as far as Gerald Foster's concerned.' Lambert received this gobbet of information in silence.

Maggie finished the doughnut and washed it down with a long draught of tea. 'She says he's not keyed into the sex bit. The female form is not what makes him tick.' She picked up the second doughnut. 'It's business. Money. Success.'

'Your sister is a sound judge?' Lambert said.

She widened her pale grey eyes. 'None better.' She tucked the stray wisp into the knot on top of her head. 'Be advised,' she said with authority. 'By them as knows.'

CHAPTER 13

Monday morning was damp and overcast. Chief Inspector Kelsey had managed to dodge every feeler that had threatened to interfere with the Norfolk trip. He'd evaded and twisted, made rings round the truth, parried and prevaricated.

No one but Sergeant Lambert knew where he was bound for. Officially he was in three other places, engaged in hard slog on three separate cases. None of the places was Longmarsh, Norfolk. And none of the cases was the Foster case which no longer had official existence.

The Chief had prepared himself for the journey by putting on a longer and thicker vest made of a denser and more invulnerable mixture of fibres that offered some hope of keeping the cold out of his lower back.

He'd seen what happened to other men's backs as they advanced through life, and if vests and keeping the spine straight and the knees bent when lifting was going to assist the Chief towards a sprightly and vigorous old age, then vests and the squatting position it was going to be.

He got into the passenger seat beside Lambert. He patted his pockets to make sure he'd forgotten nothing. As fodder for the journey he'd provided himself with half a dozen washed carrots, two apples, three pears, a packet of nuts and a brown paper bag of raisins. Beautiful large sticky raisins which he'd only recently discovered in a health-food store, very different from the small dry supermarket variety in cellophane packs. He closed his eyes for a moment at the thought of the delicious muscatel taste of those exquisite delicacies.

'Bloody cold in Norfolk,' he said as they pulled out of the forecourt. 'If my memory serves me.' He'd been to

Norfolk once in his life at the age of eight. He remembered it as a wild waste of sea marshes with horses cobbled out there in the wreathing mists. 'The houses are never built foursquare,' he said, looking back into that long-ago series of snapshots in his brain. 'The front door is never bang in the middle, it's always round a corner.' It had given the dwellings a withdrawn, hidden character, he'd felt there was some primitive mystery in the Norfolk wastes, some secret the inhabitants were certainly not sharing with holidaying outsiders.

Sergeant Lambert had never set foot in East Anglia. To him it meant boats and inland waterways, a great many churches and a cold wind blowing in from the North Sea.

'I hope we're not going to have a wasted journey,' he said. At least they knew they'd find Hetty Attwood alive and living with her sister—a Mrs Webb—at The Old Bakery. Not that they had advised the ladies of their coming. But Norwich had confirmed that the sisters were there, neither stretched out in a mortuary nor gallivanting in Spain.

As they pulled out into the road the Chief half glanced back, against his better judgment. He saw the swing doors open violently and the desk sergeant rush out, waving a paper at him. But the Chief betrayed by not a muscle that he'd seen the delaying summons. He glanced resolutely ahead again.

'We should make good time,' he said to Lambert. He settled back into his seat. 'Could be there by lunch time.'

A fine rain was falling as they approached Longmarsh on the coast road. It was little more than a hamlet, a string of cottages along the shore, a petrol station, a post office and stores, a church on a sentinel hill looking down at the village.

The Old Bakery was a flint-cobble dwelling of considerable antiquity and charm; it stood on a little rise near the shore.

Mrs Webb opened the door to them. She was a small sturdy woman of sixty-three or -four, with a fresh cheerful face, sharp bright eyes so dark brown they looked almost black. Her skin was olive and her hair thick and abundant, looped up behind her ears in black coils liberally streaked with grey.

'Yes?' She looked up at them with a smile, not at all put out by the sudden appearance of two great hulking strangers on her doorstep. Lambert got the impression she was a friendly, chatty type who would welcome any visitor, most of all, perhaps, tall well-built men, putting her in mind maybe of her late husband, the fisherman drowned in the floods.

Kelsey explained that they'd come in connection with the recent death of Miss Hetty Attwood's late mistress, that there was nothing to agitate Miss Attwood, although naturally she would be distressed to hear of Mrs Foster's death. There were one or two details they felt Miss Attwood might be able to help them with as she'd known the deceased lady so long and so well.

As they'd suspected, the news of Vera's death was a surprise at The Old Bakery. Kelsey didn't elaborate, he would wait for that till he was face to face with Hetty. 'She will be upset,' Mrs Webb said, shaking her head. 'She was that devoted to her Miss Vera.'

She had never met Vera herself but she'd heard much about the dwellers at Lynwood and felt herself to be acquainted with the family.

She led the two men into the hall. Sinister stains marked the walls of the ground-floor rooms high up near the ceilings. 'Flood marks,' Mrs Webb said in a tone of pride. 'We don't use the ground floor now for anything but storage. It's better that way.'

Safer, she means, Lambert thought, imagining the

fierce dark surge of waters gathering all in a moment, curling in round the edge of the marshes, racing into a single obliterating circle, a great icy sweep. He blew out a long breath.

Mrs Webb led the way up to the first floor. 'My sister's taking it easy today,' she said. It seemed Hetty had a cold, was keeping indoors for the present.

'If you wouldn't mind waiting a moment,' Mrs Webb said. 'I'll speak to her first, tell her the sad news, give her time to calm herself.' She opened a door leading into a long sitting-room looking out over the salt marshes. Kelsey heard her soft tones explaining, sympathizing, the low sound of a woman crying. After a few minutes Mrs Webb beckoned them into the room.

Hetty was resting on a sofa with a rug wrapped round her. She resembled her sister in colouring, but looked plumper, heavier of build. Her dark eyes were shrewd and intelligent. She was dabbing at her cheeks with a handkerchief when they came up to the sofa.

'It's been a shock for you,' Kelsey said. 'I'm very sorry, it couldn't be helped.'

She gave a nod and a sigh. 'I'm all right now.'

Mrs Webb bustled forward with chairs. 'Do sit down. And I'm sure you'd like some tea after your drive? Or coffee? It wouldn't take a moment.'

Kelsey settled for coffee. While it was being prepared Mrs Webb kept darting back into the room to hear what was being said. She reminded Sergeant Lambert of a coal-tit dabbing at a bag of nuts hung up in the garden.

The Chief explained the circumstances of Vera Foster's death, the findings of the inquest. Hetty shed fresh tears but seemed able to accept without difficulty the verdict of suicide. 'She tried that once before,' she said in tones of distress. 'It was me that found her. Me and Mr Foster, after her father's funeral.'

No, there had been no letter on that occasion, no note,

no communication of any kind. She was quite certain, there was no possibility that she could have been mistaken.

Kelsey told her about the card that had been lying under Vera's fingers, the words that had been under-lined. Had there been anything at all like that before, anything that could in any way have been construed as an indirect form of communication — even if not recognized as such at the time?

No, there had been nothing like that, she was sure of it. She'd run into the room a few feet ahead of Mr Foster. She'd at once run over to the bed, snatched up Miss Vera's hand, felt the pulse, tried to rouse her.

Kelsey took her over the ground a second and a third time but he couldn't shake her.

'Poor Miss Vera.' Hetty plucked at the surface of the rug tucked round her. 'She used to get very depressed sometimes. She always did miss her daddy, she never got over losing him.' Her fingers became more agitated, she pulled off little pills of wool. 'It doesn't do to be too fond of anyone in this life, it takes too much getting over when you lose them.'

The Chief asked if there were any other keys to the principal bedroom. She thought about it but couldn't recall ever seeing a spare key to either door, or hearing anyone mention such a key. 'But I do remember there were some odd keys in a drawer in the kitchen dresser,' she said, wrinkling her brow. 'Old keys, they were always there, I never bothered to find out where they belonged.'

Kelsey didn't persist. Easy enough for Foster to have another key cut if need be in the course of his business trips, and no one any the wiser.

'You left Lynwood in the spring,' he said.

'Yes, I left in April.'

'Hetty never took that brooch,' Mrs Webb suddenly said with passion. She darted a look from one man to the other. 'I suppose you've heard about that.' She paused as a thought struck her. 'Is that what you've come about? Is there something missing? Some of Mrs Foster's jewellery?'

Kelsey shook his head and a look of profound relief settled over Mrs Webb's features. 'Someone else took that brooch,' she said. 'Hetty told me all about it.'

Kelsey looked enquiringly at Hetty. 'I've been over it time and again in my mind,' she said. 'All I know is I didn't take the brooch.' She smiled faintly. 'I did take other things, I'll admit to that. Just little things over the years, things that didn't matter or were going to be thrown out anyway.' She gave him a slanting look from her dark eyes. 'People don't value things the way I do.'

'And Mrs Foster — Miss Vera — she knew about those little oddments,' Kelsey said delicately.

She gave a brisk nod. 'Of course she did. She'd known ever since she was a child. Children know pretty well everything that goes on in a house.' She gave him a direct look. 'Her father knew about it too. Miss Vera told on me once when she was a child, when I'd been severe with her after she'd been naughty.' She glanced aside. 'She was always capable of that. A streak of spite. But it made no difference to what I felt for her. I loved her all the same.'

She looked back again at the Chief. 'Mr Murdoch didn't mind, he didn't attach any importance to the odds and ends. I heard what he said to Miss Vera when she told him.' She caught Kelsey's expression and grinned openly at him. 'Oh yes, I've listened at doors in my time. Everyone does in private service.'

She gazed at him with half-mischievous challenge. 'I daresay you policemen have a trick or two you're not publishing in the newspapers.'

Her face lost its half-smiling look. 'But Miss Vera knew full well there was a strict limit to what I'd take.' She put a hand up to her face. 'That's what really upset me about the brooch. She must have known I'd never take it. A valuable piece of jewellery. And it belonged to her dear dead mother that I'd loved and nursed and seen laid in the ground.'

She closed her eyes for a moment. 'She let Mr Foster say I took it, she let him accuse me.' She drew a deep quivering breath. 'I didn't want to stay on after that. It took the heart out of me.'

'How do you think the brooch came to be among your things?' Kelsey asked.

'I've thought about that many a time,' she said with renewed vigour. 'And my belief is it could have been Alma Driscoll who put it there.' She raised her hand. 'Mind, I'm not saying it definitely was Alma, for I've never actually known the girl to thieve. But it could have been her. She knew about the brooch, she'd seen it once or twice when Miss Vera took it out, she knew where it was kept.'

'Why would she put it among your things?'

'I can think of two different reasons,' Hetty said at once. 'She could have been short of cash, she could have stolen the brooch intending to sell it. But Miss Vera found out it was missing before she had time to sell it, so rather than have it found in her things she slipped it in among mine. She knew full well they'd believe I'd taken it a lot quicker than they'd believe she had.'

'And the other possibility?'

'Alma always had her eye on the housekeeper's job, right from the day she first set foot in Lynwood. I'm sure she thought I'd be gone pretty soon, either of my own free will or given the push by Mr Foster. But things didn't turn out that way, I stayed on.' She touched her chin. 'I think in the end she may have decided she'd have to take a hand in it if she was ever going to get me out, she'd have to work out some way of getting me the sack. So she took the brooch simply in order to have it found among my things.'

She moved her hand. 'I was out of Lynwood before I really gathered my wits about me. It was afterwards, here, that I've had time to think about it all, try to work out what could have happened.' She jerked her head emphatically. 'It wasn't me that took the brooch so it must have been Alma. It couldn't have been anyone else.'

'You don't like Alma,' the Chief said.

She pulled down the corners of her mouth. 'I don't dislike her. But it's difficult to be fond of someone that's after your job. And things were a bit heated at the last. I didn't exactly kiss any of them goodbye.' She shrugged. 'But take her all round, Alma's well enough in her way. She's a good worker, a good cook. She's too free and easy in her ways to suit my taste, she's what you'd call a bit flashy and common.'

She inclined her head at the Chief. 'Mr Foster didn't like that, he mentioned it to me more than once. He caught Alma bringing one of her boy-friends into Lynwood not long after she started work, slipping him at the side door and up the back stairs late in the evening. Mr Foster soon gave her what for, told her what she did away from the house was one thing but what she did inside Lynwood was his business. He was as strict in his ways about that sort of thing,' she said with approval, 'as ever old Mr Murdoch was. And Miss Vera, she wouldn't have allowed anything like that either. Not that Mr Foster told her about it, he never wanted to upset her. He just mentioned it to me, told me to keep an eye on Alma but not to go worrying Miss Vera about it.'

She cocked a shrewd eye at the Chief. 'Mr Foster never had a girl-friend before Miss Vera. He was twenty-six years old when they were married and I doubt if he'd ever taken a lassie out before.'

She saw the Chief's sceptical look. 'You may look like that, I may be a spinster but I'm no stranger to the ways of the world. It was always separate rooms at Lynwood, right from the day they were married. Mr Foster isn't a physical man, if you take my meaning, isn't now and never was.'

She made a little inclination of her head. 'That suited Miss Vera fine. I used to think that was one of the chief reasons she married him. She was never one for the lads, always her daddy's lassie. Her father spoiled her and so did I, there's no denying it. She was such a pretty little thing. And her poor mother dying the way she did, it was only natural we should fuss over her. We always treated her as if she was a bit delicate so she grew up thinking of herself that way, worried about her health and so on.'

She sighed. 'It got worse as she got older. She didn't take kindly to the fact that she wasn't a slip of a girl any more. She started to coddle herself worse than ever.'

There was another brief silence. 'How did you get on with Mr Foster?' Kelsey asked before Hetty could slip back into tears.

'Well enough. He's a very decent sort of man.'

'I believe you knew him as a lad?'

'That I did,' she said with energy. 'That was how he came to be taken on by Mr Murdoch. I knew the family, very decent hard-working folk. It was a crying shame when the lad had to be put in an orphanage, his poor father and mother would have turned in their graves from the shame of it if they'd known.

'Mr Murdoch asked the orphanage if they had a lad that might make a clerk and they suggested four or five boys and he saw them all. He said to me: This Foster lad seems likely enough, he tells me was a Cannonbridge lad originally, do you know anything about the family? I was able to tell him the boy had a decent background, the father was a shop manager and the mother was a very nice kind of creature, a bit gentle and helpless but as honest as the day.

'I told Mr Murdoch: If you want a decent hard-working

honest lad, the Foster lad will be your man. So he took him on. He wanted a boy that would work without someone looking over his shoulder all the time.'

She widened her eyes at the Chief. 'And Mr Foster certainly worked. You never in your life saw a lad the like of him for working. From the day he went into Mr Murdoch's little office down in the town he worked like a demon. He used to come up to the house as well, of course, Mr Murdoch often did paperwork at Lynwood.

'And of course Mr Foster used to see Miss Vera about the place. Not that they were sweethearts or anything like that, but they got used to each other, she got to trust him.

'Then when Mr Murdoch died so sudden, Mr Foster was a great help to Miss Vera. Natural enough they should get married. Miss Vera was always one to rely on a man, brought up to it, you see, and Mr Foster was there, so she married him. It worked very well. I don't think she ever had a day's worry from him. Which is more,' she added grimly, 'than most women can say for their husbands.'

She dabbed away a tear. 'Whatever it was that brought her to do away with herself I'm sure it was nothing Mr Foster did. Mr Murdoch thought very highly indeed of him. He'd have been delighted to know he married Miss Vera, he'd have felt sure she was in good hands. And the business too, Mr Murdoch couldn't have wished for a better man to take it over.'

'Mr Foster treated Hetty very fairly about money,' Mrs Webb put in. She glanced at her sister. 'You should make that clear to the Chief Inspector, it's only fair to Mr Foster.'

'Well, yes,' Hetty agreed. 'I always found him a very fair man. I suppose he did really believe I took that brooch. I can't altogether blame him for that, he didn't know me the way Miss Vera did, not really know me.' She looked up at the Chief. 'He made an investment for me, a sort of pension.'

'And a nice little investment it is,' Mrs Webb said. 'Government stock. Absolutely safe and brings in a good sum twice a year.'

As they were standing up to leave, Hetty suddenly glanced up at them and said, 'Why have you driven all this way?'

'To clear everything up, dear,' Mrs Webb said. 'To get it all straight in their minds.'

'That's about it,' the Chief said heartily. 'And you've both been of great assistance.'

The rain had stopped when they took the road back to Cannonbridge. A soft gold light shone out over the marshes. In the distance Lambert heard the hollow call of a marsh bird.

'Strikes me,' Kelsey said, settling back into his seat, 'that it wasn't Hetty that swiped that brooch. Nor Alma Driscoll. It was Master Gerald Foster. It was he that drew Vera's attention to the brooch, showed her the picture in the magazine, sent her looking in her bureau.'

He stared ahead at the grey road. 'There's very much the same pattern about Vera's death and the theft of the brooch. If Foster arranged both happenings then you could expect to find the same pattern.'

He screwed up his face. 'Foster takes an existing fact, well-known, indisputable. Fact one: Vera's first attempt at suicide. Fact two: Hetty's well-known habit of nicking stuff. Then he exaggerates each of these, in the hope that everyone will swallow the exaggerations as easily as they swallowed the original facts. Exaggeration one: Vera goes one step further and this time actually succeeds in killing herself. Exaggeration two: Hetty goes one step further and this time steals a really valuable object. Everyone accepts both occurrences at face value, both are very similar to what they positively know has happened before, just a few degrees more so in each case. And in my opinion both occurrences were deceptions, rigged by the same hand, Master Foster.'

'That business of the letter,' Lambert said. 'It seems certain now there was no letter the first time and no form of indirect communication.'

'Which all goes to confirm my opinion,' Kelsey said stoutly. 'If Vera really intended to kill herself she'd have acted as she did before, simply go upstairs, take a massive overdose, lie down just as she was, close her eyes and wait to die, not go fooling about with photographs and picture postcards. Foster knew that, but he couldn't leave well alone, he had to underline everything, dress up the scene, make absolutely certain we'd all swallow the death as suicide.' He grunted. 'And it worked. We did all swallow it.'

'Maybe,' Lambert said despairingly, 'there was nothing to swallow, she simply behaved differently both times. She doesn't strike me as a woman who'd always be totally consistent in what she did. She was in a very different situation at both attempts. The first time she'd just received a sudden overwhelming blow, the second time she was quite a bit older, suffering from a long, slow, insidious depression. She could have been brooding about taking her own life, worked out exactly what she'd do.'

Kelsey struck his fists together. 'There's no comparison between the two occasions. On the one hand you have swift decisive action, on the other theatricality, props. Two totally different atmospheres because the work of two totally different personalities.' He gave a mighty yawn. 'The trouble with Foster, he never quite knows where to draw the line. Lack of judgment, that's where they all fall down in the end.' He settled back and closed his eyes.

Some time later, when Lambert believed the Chief to be asleep, Kelsey suddenly said, 'I think we've got enough now to warrant a word with Miss Jordan.'

'Now?' Lambert echoed, startled out of his absorption in the question of what time he would be eating his supper.

'Not today,' Kelsey said. 'Tomorrow, maybe. Or the day after.' He intended to sleep on it. He would know when he woke in the morning if he was going over to Wychford to put one or two questions to Edith Jordan.

'Either she can answer them satisfactorily or she can't,' he said. A few very straightforward questions. As for instance: How did she propose to finance the purchase of the business she was seeking? Why did she leave the Elgood job so abruptly?

'And why,' Sergeant Lambert said, having independently pursued the same line of thought, 'didn't she put the porridge in the Aga on that Thursday night?'

CHAPTER 14

When the morning light hit the Chief in the eyeballs next day his first waking thought was: Go ahead, ask her. That settled the matter as far as he was concerned. Now the only question was when.

In the event it was two days before he found the time. It wasn't something he wished to slot in between a couple of meetings, he had to be free to devote his mind—and his time—to it for the entire half of one day.

'Tomorrow morning,' he said to Sergeant Lambert. 'Over to Wychford.' Provided no cataclysm hit Cannonbridge before morning.

At nine o'clock next day the Chief put his head down and left the station at a rapid pace, with Lambert half a step behind, guarding his rear.

They made the forecourt without any successful attack

from the forces of interruption and delay. They reached the car.

'Get cracking,' Kelsey said as soon as he was halfway into the passenger seat.

At the other end of the forecourt a car was turning in. It looked very like the Super's car. Lambert began to pull out and Kelsey stooped so that his head was only half visible.

Two minutes later they were safely out on the road, travelling at the maximum permitted speed in the direction of Wychford, and the Super was stepping out on to the forecourt and glancing about for the Chief's car which had been there—surely?—half a moment before.

Orchard House lay a good half-mile outside Wychford. The school consisted of a group of buildings of various dates set around a central edifice—a mansion of grey granite erected a good hundred years ago by a wealthy iron and steel merchant. He had succeeded in business and then set about the much more formidable task of passing himself off as a gentleman.

After his death Orchard House had been turned into a girls' school, extended as time went by. It was expensive, exclusive, highly successful.

Lambert turned the car in through the tall wrought-iron gates. Beautifully kept gravel paths led off from a central turning circle in front of an imposing entrance with wide shallow stone steps and a pillared portico.

An air of peace enveloped the place, not the silence of neglect or isolation, but the near-silence of disciplined and purposeful activity carried on in an atmosphere of authority and security. Lambert began to feel hypnotized by that brooding calm.

Himself a product of a minor—very minor—public school, he felt again the old sense of reassurance, of a universe proceeding along rational and orderly lines. It seemed a very long way from Cannonbridge.

A stream of girls carrying lacrosse stricks came out of a side entrance and went off along one of the paths in the direction of vast playing-fields.

The two men walked in silence to the front door. Lambert pressed the bell and they were admitted by a uniformed maid.

Yes, she would inform the headmistress that Chief Inspector Kelsey would be grateful if she could spare him a moment. Yes, she believed the headmistress was free at present, in her study. If they would care to step inside she wouldn't keep them a moment.

Lambert followed the Chief into a spacious circular hall with a marble floor and an ornate ceiling with elegant cornice work. A fine staircase rose out of the hall, curving up to balustraded landings and white-painted corridors. A distant murmur of voices, the ring of a phone bell, rhythmic sounds of someone working in the gardens, the chirrup of birds . . . Lambert felt his eyelids begin to droop.

The headmistress came briskly towards them along a passage leading from the rear of the ground floor. A short woman in her forties, strongly built; she wore a good tweed suit and looked as if she enjoyed a game of golf. She had a professional, faintly smiling look, eyes of hawklike keenness, a slightly tanned skin; her short greying hair was well cut and waved.

She inclined her head as the Chief explained that he was asking permission to speak to a member of the Orchard House staff. He couldn't say how long he would keep the lady but he would do his best not to detain her longer than was necessary. No, he was very sorry, but he couldn't give any indication of the nature of his business.

The headmistress's eyes clearly registered the fact that it would have been very simple for the Chief to say: No, it's nothing serious, nothing for you to worry about, but that he did not in fact utter those simple words.

At the mention of the name of the member of staff the headmistress's face expressed momentary surprise, replaced at once by her habitual look of detached ease and good-natured control.

'Miss Jordan,' she said on a reflective note. 'Yes, certainly, I'll have one of the maids send her along to you. If you'll follow me I'll show you where you can talk to her.' She led the way along a passage.

'We've been very satisfied with Miss Jordan's work,' she observed in a light easy tone as she halted at a closed door. 'She's fitted in here very well indeed.'

She threw open the door. She turned and levelled a look at the Chief. 'If she were looking for a permanent post — which she tells me she is not — I should be most happy to offer her one.' She waved them into the room and departed along the corridor. It seemed to Lambert that he had just been listening to a testimonial delivered on Miss Jordan's behalf like a pronouncement from an Eastern potentate, beside which such airy trifles as vague suspicions, uneasy doubts and deep-down feelings in the bones might be reckoned as of very little consequence indeed.

The Chief didn't sit down, but walked over to the window and stood looking out at the gardens, brilliant with michaelmas daisies, chrysanthemums, dahlias. Smoothly sloping lawns, dark banks of shrubs, clusters of berries, scarlet, white and purple. A gardener stooped over a rose bed with secateurs in his hand.

Sergeant Lambert dropped into an easy chair and closed his eyes. He was almost asleep when he heard light, measured steps along the passage.

The door opened and Edith Jordan came in. She looked very poised, very trim in a dark tailored dress. Lambert got to his feet and the Chief walked across from the window as she closed the door and turned to face them with a clear, impersonal gaze.

'Ah, yes, Chief Inspector Kelsey,' she said, with an air as of recognizing an acquaintance at some public occasion. 'And Sergeant Lambert.' She gave him a brief nod and stood waiting with a look of courteous enquiry.

The Chief didn't tell her he'd called on some trifling matter that would occupy only a few minutes of her time, he didn't tell her not to be in any way alarmed by his visit. He didn't smile at her as they all sat down. And Miss Jordan's clear hazel eyes noted these omissions.

'Well now, Chief Inspector,' she said when they were all three seated, all three upright and alert in posture. 'What can I do for you?'

'I have a couple of questions to ask you,' Kelsey said in a tone from which lightness was markedly absent.

'Go ahead and ask them,' she said in a cooperative manner. She gave the merest glance at her wristwatch.

'These questions,' the Chief said, 'arise from the death of Mrs Vera Foster.'

She looked at him with surprise. 'Surely the verdict of the inquest —'

'Such a verdict,' Kelsey said, 'doesn't necessarily mean the files are closed once and for all.'

He gave her a level look. 'I should be glad of a satisfactory explanation to one or two matters that have been puzzling me.' She moved her head slightly in acquiescence.

'You were employed,' the Chief said, 'as a temporary help by a Mr and Mrs Elgood, between August 23rd and September 2nd.' She gave a nod. 'Mrs Elgood asked you to stay on for an extra week and you agreed. Then you abruptly changed your mind and left on the date you'd originally settled. Why was that?'

'I didn't particularly want to stay on,' she said with a faint smile. 'My room was small and cramped, the bed was fearfully uncomfortable, the mattress was old and lumpy. I didn't have one good night's sleep while I was there. I didn't wish to hurt their feelings by mentioning this; they were kind, decent people who'd done their best to make me feel at home, but frankly, the prospect of another week in that room—' She gave a little sigh. 'I had an exceptionally comfortable home at Fairhaven, I fear it spoiled me for more spartan conditions.'

'But you did agree to stay on at first,' Kelsey persisted. 'Why? If you were so anxious to get away?'

She shook her head. 'No, I didn't actually agree. I said I'd stay on if the agency had no objections. I confidently expected Miss Unwin to say she needed me for another job. I knew the Elgoods could manage without me if they had to.'

She smiled again. 'But to my dismay Miss Unwin told Mrs Elgood it was all right by her, I could stay on for the extra week. I thought about it, whether I could perhaps grit my teeth and stay on after all, but after another night on that dreadful bed with the farm animals and fowl tuning up in the early morning—' She shook her head. 'I made up some excuse next day. I didn't want to be rude so I said a personal matter had cropped up and I was sorry, I wouldn't be able to stay on after all.

'I told Mrs Elgood I'd be grateful if she'd just accept that without referring the matter again to Miss Unwin. I didn't want the agency to think I was becoming moody or whimsical about my postings. Mrs Elgood was very nice about it, she said she quite understood.'

'Did your sudden change of mind have anything to do with a phone call you received at the Elgoods?'

'Phone call?' she echoed with a slight frown.

'You received a phone call on the Thursday before you left the Elgoods. It was immediately after the call that you told Mrs Elgood you'd changed your mind and would be leaving on the Saturday as you'd originally agreed.'

'My decision had nothing to do with any phone call. It

was as I've just told you, I wasn't comfortable there.'

'Who was the call from?'

'I haven't the faintest idea,' she said with spirit. 'After all these weeks you expect me to remember a single phone call?'

'It was the only call you received at the Elgoods apart from the calls from the agency. I would imagine you could recall who made it.'

She frowned down at the carpet. 'Yes,' she said after a moment. 'As a matter of fact I can. It was probably my cousin in Bridport. I believe she did ring me at the Elgoods.'

'The call was from a man.'

'Then that would be my cousin's husband. Yes, I remember, he did speak to me first. They'd been asking me to go and stay with them for a holiday, we'd been trying to arrange a date.'

'And have you fixed a date?'

'Yes. I'm spending Christmas with them.'

'I understand,' Kelsey said with an abrupt change of tack, 'that you intend to set up a small business of your own?'

'I do.' She showed no surprise at the sudden switch.

'May I ask how you intend to finance the purchase of this business?'

She moved her head with an air of anger.

'Believe me,' the Chief said, 'I'm not asking these questions out of idle curiosity.'

'I intend to finance the purchase with a loan,' she said in clipped tones.

'May I ask who is going to make the loan?'

There was a brief silence, then she said, 'I most strongly object to the personal nature of these questions but I will answer you none the less. The loan is to be made by Mr Foster. Mr Gerald Foster of Lynwood.'

CHAPTER 15

'I see,' Kelsey said. 'And what is the size of the loan?'

'It's not settled yet. It depends on what I have to pay for the business.'

'And when did Mr Foster agree to make this loan?'

'That sounds as if I approached Mr Foster and asked him for a loan,' she objected. 'I did not. He offered to make me the loan if I needed one.'

'May I ask what were the circumstances in which he made this offer?'

She gave him a long look before she answered. 'Mrs Foster admired some things I'd made, blouses, lingerie and so on. I told her I'd always wanted to set up in business on my own but I'd gone into it and discovered it would need too much capital. We were just chatting, it was about a week after I went to Lynwood. I certainly had no idea what the conversation would lead to.

'She was very interested. She talked about it later to her husband; she told him she thought she might back me, advance me the capital. She would want to have some say in the business. She felt she needed a new interest and this was something that appealed to her. She asked him what he thought of the idea.'

'And what did he think of it?'

'He encouraged her, he thought it would do her good. Of course, everything would have to be gone into properly, drawn up legally and so on.'

'When did you first start looking for a business?'

'I made some enquiries while I was still at Fairhaven, soon after Mrs Lydiatt died. I was thinking about what I would do, and I thought if ever I was to start out on my own that might be the time to try. I rang various agencies to see what sort of money was needed to buy the kind of premises I wanted.'

'At that time how were you intending to finance the purchase?'

She smiled slightly. 'I fear I was a trifle optimistic. I thought I could manage the whole sum myself. I had no idea how the value of property had risen, I never had anything to do with property. I'd been left a little money from my mother. I'd invested that and it had grown quite a bit. Then I'd saved the bulk of my salary at Fairhaven. Mrs Lydiatt paid me well and I've never been extravagant. Then of course Mrs Lydiatt left me some money in her will.'

'A good deal less than you expected,' Kelsey said.

'Why should you think that?' she said on a note of surprise. 'I knew precisely what Mrs Lydiatt was going to leave me, she made no secret of the amount. She told me at the time the will was drawn up. I certainly didn't expect more, I thought it very generous of her. Altogether I had about twelve or thirteen thousand pounds, I imagined that would be enough, I thought it a very handsome sum.'

She smiled again. 'I got a shock when I discovered current prices.' She sighed. 'But I couldn't bear to lose my dream for good, so I left my name on the agents' books. I thought it just possible some run-down little place might turn up where the owner needed to sell in a hurry, or an estate had to be wound up. I could, after all, offer cash, even if it wasn't a great deal.'

She moved her hand. 'And I thought if a suitable business did turn up at a figure that was only a couple of thousand more than I had, then perhaps I could persuade my bank to lend me the balance and I could repay them out of profits. In the meantime I was going to take temporary posts and save every penny I could. I thought I'd give it two years. If I didn't find anything in that time I'd abandon the idea and take a permanent job.

'By the time I went to Lynwood I was coming to the conclusion that it was pretty hopeless. There was nothing even faintly possible at anything like my sort of money.'

'So you made this arrangement with Mrs Foster.'

'Yes. I was then able to give the estate agents definite instructions.'

'And after Mrs Foster died — the arrangement still stood?'

'Yes. Mr Foster said he was grateful for what I'd been able to do for his wife. He felt she would have wished him to go on with the loan. I'll pay interest or a share of the profits, whatever's decided, that's all still to be gone into. The capital will be repaid on my death — after the sale of the business. I've no dependants or close relatives, it's all perfectly straightforward. He doesn't require any hand in running the business as his wife would have done.'

'You stayed on at Lynwood for some time after Mrs Foster's death,' Kelsey observed.

'Mr Foster asked me to, and it was the obvious course. I helped to keep things running, he could scarcely have managed without some assistance. It was a very difficult time for him, he was very grateful.'

'You seem to get on well with him.'

'Very well,' she said at once. 'Right from the first time we met at Fairhaven —'

'At Fairhaven?' he repeated in a tone that was almost a whisper.

She smiled. 'Of course I meant Lynwood. I spoke of Fairhaven just now, it was still in my mind.'

'I think, in fact, you did meet Mr Foster at Fairhaven,' Kelsey said in the same gentle tone.

'No, I did not. I met him at Lynwood when I went there to work.'

'There was a building plot for sale at Fairhaven. I believe Mr Foster went over to see it.'

'I know nothing about that. He certainly never mentioned it to me.'

'Wasn't it your job to show prospective purchasers over the plot?'

She shook her head. 'The agent saw to that. I sometimes showed people over the house if the agent couldn't manage to be there, but mostly he came over for that too.'

'Why didn't you make Mrs Foster's porridge that last night?' Kelsey asked abruptly.

'Porridge?' She seemed thrown off her stride by this swift change of direction.

'When Alma returned to Lynwood that Friday morning she looked in the Aga and found you hadn't put the porridge in to cook. Why not?'

She seemed at a loss. 'I thought I did put it in.'

'Alma is positive you did not. You're a reliable, careful woman, you pay great attention to detail. You made the porridge the previous time Alma was away. She reminded you about it before she went off duty that Thursday afternoon. But you didn't make it. Why not?'

She frowned. 'I do remember I was very tired that evening. I went to bed as soon as I'd attended to Mrs Foster.' She moved her shoulders. 'The porridge wasn't part of my normal duties, I was anxious to get to bed, I must have forgotten it.'

'Did you sleep so heavily because you'd taken a sleeping pill?'

'I never take sleeping pills.' She smiled slightly. 'My difficulty has always been waking up in the mornings, not getting to sleep at night.'

'You slept throughout that night, you heard nothing, you didn't wake for any reason?'

'That is so.'

'That is what you stated at the inquest.'

'It is.'

He's going to have to drop it, Lambert thought, he'll

have to accept the fact that he's mistaken in all this, he's been mistaken all along, he never had anything to go on except a hunch. She's given eminently reasonable answers to every question he's asked.

There was a brief silence, then Miss Jordan looked at her watch. 'If there's nothing else, Chief Inspector, I've a number of duties to attend to.'

Kelsey looked at her for several moments. 'I'm going to ask you if you'd be good enough to come along with us now to Cannonbridge,' he said at last. 'There are one or two questions I'd like to put to Mr Foster in your presence. You're at liberty to refuse, but I'd appreciate it if you would come.'

She closed her eyes for an instant. 'Is it really necessary?' she said with an air of weariness.

'I wouldn't ask if I didn't believe it was.'

She gave an audible sigh. 'Very well. But I must speak to the headmistress first.' Kelsey gave a nod and she rose and left the room.

He said nothing when the door closed behind her. He sat leaning forward in his chair, striking his fists against each other. He frowned, stared down at the carpet, bit his lips, wrinkled his eyes.

Lambert knew well that in this mood the Chief didn't welcome interruption. But he must say something, he couldn't stand by and let him gallop on, if not towards disaster then in all probability towards a highly unpleasant situation resulting in reprimands and apologies all round, a good deal of humiliating biting of the dust.

He braced his shoulders. 'Miss Jordan instructed the agents on September 18th,' he said. 'Three days before Mrs Foster died.'

The Chief shot him a fierce upward glance. 'So?'

'That surely accords with her story that Mrs Foster offered her a loan. And if she was to get the loan from Mrs Foster, then surely that destroys any suggestion of a

motive for her to assist Foster to murder his wife. If it
wasn't to get the money to set herself up in business, what
other conceivable reason could she have for agreeing to
take part in the cold-blooded murder of a total stranger?'

'I don't for one moment suppose Mrs Foster ever heard
of the business venture,' Kelsey said. 'Let alone offering to
lend her the money.'

'You can't get away from the fact that she instructed
the agents three days before Mrs Foster's death. Surely if
the money was to come from Foster it would depend on
the successful carrying out of the murder. She wouldn't
be in a position to instruct the agents till after Mrs Foster's
death.'

Kelsey gave him a sour look. 'It would have been lunacy
to wait till Mrs Foster was dead before giving definite instructions. That would take some explaining later on if
questions came to be asked.'

He struck the arm of his chair. 'They had to guard
against the very thing that's happening now, questions
being asked. They had to have their answers ready. They
had to tailor their actions and the sequence in which
those actions were carried out in the light of what might
one day be asked.

'They're both intelligent, they weren't going to fall into
obvious traps. If they agreed that in the event of detailed
questioning they would say that Mrs Foster had offered
the loan, then Miss Jordan must act throughout in
accordance with that. She must give instructions before
Vera's death, not after it. And in what way would Foster
stand to lose anything by that? If something went wrong
and the murder was not successfully carried out, then
Miss Jordan wouldn't be paid her fee. All Foster would
have to do would be to tell her so, tell her to countermand
the instructions to the agents. Simple enough.'

'But all her answers could be no more than the plain
truth,' Lambert protested. 'You never even consider that.

She's a highly respectable woman, everyone we've spoken to who's had any kind of dealings with her has the greatest regard for her, there's never been anything against her in the whole of her life. But your position from first to last is that she's telling lies. You can't prove she is, you simply start from that basis with no better backing than one look exchanged between her and Foster.'

Kelsey stuck out his jaw. 'That look is enough for me.'

'But you could be mistaken in the meaning of that look. Foster might only have been signalling: "Thank goodness it's all over, what a relief! Don't you worry about your loan, I'll see to that." Miss Jordan had stayed on to help him through a bad time, he was grateful, he'd been through a very trying emotional ordeal, he'd have felt a sense of comradeship with her. Why wouldn't he smile at her when she was leaving? It seems a natural reaction to me. People smile, laugh out loud when tension relaxes. The inquest can't have been a pleasant experience for either of them, you find them a strain yourself. They were bound to feel relief when it was over.

'But you won't even consider any alternative to what you thought at that moment. You won't listen to any other explanation. You cannot possibly have been mistaken. You look down on the situation from above like the Almighty, you interpret that look once and for all. Nothing that happens afterwards or any explanation that's offered makes the slightest difference to what you imagined in that one second of time.'

The Chief said nothing. He looked back at Lambert with the mulish look the sergeant knew well. Lambert gave a sigh which he permitted to be clearly audible, he sat back in silence. When the Chief had his head down and was plunging on, the truth—if it differed from his own assessment of the facts—would always sound to him no more than a plausible explanation.

A few minutes later Miss Jordan returned. She had

slipped a coat on over her dark dress. She didn't ask how long they were likely to be, she asked no questions but walked in silence beside them out to the car. She wore no hat, and her thick dark hair with its white wings gleamed in the pale sunlight.

A little knot of girls came along a path, chattering and laughing. At the sight of Miss Jordan and the two men their faces grew curious, they craned their necks to take it in. Miss Jordan didn't glance at them, didn't look about her, but got into the rear seat as soon as Lambert opened the car door for her. Her manner showed neither tension nor irritation. She leaned back and made herself comfortable.

There was silence in the car as Lambert pulled out and headed back towards Cannonbridge. Kelsey stared out at the coppery leaves drifting down from the trees in the slight breeze.

Suddenly he sat upright. It had just struck him that the journey might be a complete waste of time. Foster might not be in his office, might not be in town at all, could have gone off on business, might be away a day or two.

He pulled a face of irritation. The whole purpose was to take Foster by surprise. If they were forced to turn the car round and drive Miss Jordan back to Wychford there was no way he could set up the confrontation another day without it going off like a damp squib. Edith Jordan would get in touch with Foster, let him know what was in the wind—whether the pair of them were innocent or guilty.

He leaned back again in his seat. Nothing he could do about it now. Ten minutes later, when they reached the office in Bridge Street, he told Lambert to stay in the car while he went inside.

Miss Greatbach was on the phone. The Chief remained standing, consumed with impatience, but with a pleasant, casual look on his face, till she'd finished. He kept his manner light and easy as he enquired for Foster.

No, Miss Greatbach told him, Mr Foster wasn't in the office, he was out at Lynwood. She didn't expect him in the office till after lunch.

Kelsey closed his eyes for a moment in relief. No, no need to phone Lynwood, he told her with a friendly smile. 'I'll just pop out there and have a word with him, I won't keep him many minutes.' The last thing he wanted was for Miss Greatbach to pick up the phone and tell Foster he was on his way.

She nodded, smiled acquiescence, picked up some papers and had begun to work on them even before the door closed behind the Chief.

He got back into the car. 'Lynwood,' he told Lambert. He offered no further word to either of them. There was silence again in the car as Lambert drove through the town and out on to the Abberley road.

Sunlight glittered the Lynwood garden as Lambert turned the car in through the gates and halted a little way along the drive. All three of them got out of the car in silence; in silence they walked towards the house and went up the front steps.

CHAPTER 16

Alma Driscoll answered Sergeant Lambert's ring at the door. She looked surprised at seeing them. In particular she seemed taken aback at the sight of Miss Jordan.

Yes, Mr Foster was in, he was working in the study, she was just about to take him some coffee.

At the sound of voices the study door opened and Foster put his head out. 'Hello, there,' he said. 'This is a surprise.' He came out into the passage.

'Come inside,' he said to the Chief. 'And Miss Jordan, I

didn't expect to see you—but do come in, all of you. You're just in time to join me in some coffee.'

Alma went off to the kitchen and Foster ushered them into the sitting-room. He asked Miss Jordan a casual question about Orchard House and she replied in the same tone. The Chief stood looking out of the window until the coffee came, then he took his seat on an upright chair.

'Now,' Foster said briskly when the door closed again behind Alma, 'what can I do for you?'

The Chief took a drink of his coffee. 'I've been wondering,' he said in a pleasant neutral tone, 'exactly why you dismissed Hetty Attwood from your service?'

'Hetty Attwood?' Foster frowned. 'Why is this? Is something wrong with Hetty?' He gave a sudden brief smile. 'She's not trying to sue me for wrongful dismissal?'

'I would be glad if you'd answer the question,' Kelsey said patiently.

'I've no objection to answering it. None at all.' Foster glanced at Miss Jordan. 'Though I can't think why you need Miss Jordan here in order to ask me about Hetty Attwood.' Kelsey gave an audible sigh but said nothing. Miss Jordan sipped her coffee, took a biscuit and began to eat it.

Foster moved his shoulders. 'Hetty was getting to be a pain in the neck,' he said abruptly. 'More so every year. My wife wouldn't dismiss her. Hetty took advantage of the position. When I first came here, when I was clerk to Mr Murdoch, long before I married Vera, I saw the way Hetty was allowed to do more or less as she pleased. Mr Murdoch left the entire running of Lynwood to her, she was a law unto herself.

'I tried to get rid of her as soon as I married Vera but it was no use. I didn't press the point, it upset my wife, so I did the next best thing. I took on another more sensible person in addition to Hetty, so at least after that the place was run a good deal more efficiently. There were difficulties, of course. Hetty resented Alma. I did hope she'd resent her to the point of packing her bags, but no such luck. If it wasn't for Alma's good sense, turning a blind eye and a deaf ear to provocation from Hetty on a great many occasions, there would have been constant rows in the kitchen.'

He gestured with one hand. 'Hetty had always helped herself to oddments, one could scarcely expect anything else, the way she was allowed to go on. One day she went too far. She took a brooch belonging to my wife, a valuable brooch. Even Vera couldn't stomach that. Technically, she wasn't sacked but somewhat forcibly retired.'

He jerked his head. 'I was extremely glad to see the back of her. I made suitable financial provision for her, of course—and very pleased I was to settle at the price. I regarded it as money well spent.'

He gave Kelsey a fierce direct look. 'There isn't a court in the land that would regard my actions as unjust—if that's what's at the bottom of this visit.'

'I put it to you,' Kelsey said, 'that you sacked Hetty in order to make way for Miss Jordan.' Foster gave an exclamation but Kelsey ignored it. 'I also put it to you that it was you who removed the brooch from your wife's desk and put it among Hetty's things. You then reminded your wife about the brooch, causing her to look it out. When she found it was missing you encouraged everyone in the belief that Hetty had taken it. You searched Hetty's belongings and of course discovered the brooch among them.'

'Why on earth would I do that?' Foster said with a face of astonishment.

'To provide a cast-iron excuse for getting rid of Hetty. So that the next time your wife was laid up with sciatica Hetty would no longer be there to nurse her. Your wife would then need to summon outside assistance and you had arranged that it would be at once forthcoming — in the shape of Miss Jordan.'

'This is totally ridiculous,' Foster said with angry protest. 'I didn't even know Miss Jordan existed when I got rid of Hetty. I'd been doing my best to get rid of her for years. If I went to the lengths of stealing a brooch to get rid of her why didn't I do it years before? Why put up with her for as long as I did?' Kelsey said nothing.

Foster looked at the Chief with incredulity. 'Are you saying I sacked Hetty to clear a path into Lynwood for a woman I hadn't even met? Whose existence I didn't even know of?'

'But you had met Miss Jordan,' Kelsey said mildly. 'You met her early in the year when you went over to Mildenhall to look at a building site. Part of the garden of a house in Hawthorn Lane; Fairhaven, the property of the late Mrs Lydiatt. Miss Jordan had worked for Mrs Lydiatt, she stayed on at Fairhaven to show people over the property. You were taken over the building plot by Miss Jordan.'

'Good God!' Foster said. 'So this is what this visitation is in aid of. I never went near any building plot in Hawthorn Lane. I remember the plot now you remind me of it. I saw it advertised but I realized its location was no good to me. I passed on the information to Ormrod, the builder; just his style. I've done that dozens of times over the years — passed the word on to Ormrod.'

He gave a short bark of a laugh. 'I see what it is. You got hold of the fact that Ormrod heard about the land from me, you've worked all this farrago back from that. Do you know,' he added, 'until this moment I had no idea that building plot was in any way connected with Miss Jordan?'

'I see no reason why Mr Foster should have known,' Miss Jordan said to Kelsey. 'I never had occasion to mention it while I was here.'

Foster made an irritated gesture. 'And surely all this was way back in the New Year. Until you mentioned Hawthorn Lane just now I'd forgotten I ever saw the advertisement. I've passed on several tips to Ormrod since then. I'd be hard put to it to give you the addresses of any of the locations.'

He got to his feet and paced about the room. 'Actually, this is pretty monstrous behaviour on your part, Chief Inspector. I don't know that I'm compelled to put up with it. You get hold of some gobbet of information and on the strength of that you go ferreting about into the dismissal of a servant months ago. You drag Miss Jordan over here from her work—what on earth for? With some dramatic idea of confronting me? What with? Precisely what is in your mind, Chief Inspector? Am I being charged with something? If so, charge me. I challenge you. If I'm supposed to have engineered the introduction of Miss Jordan into Lynwood, with what motive did I plan her introduction?'

Kelsey said nothing but sat looking at his cup with a face wiped clear of expression.

Foster thrust at the air with his fist. 'And let me tell you, if you've been going round asking questions that would in any way cast any kind of shadow across my name or reputation either in this town or anywhere else—you'll find that the law is a two-edged weapon. You can feel the weight of it as well as the next citizen. More so, if there's any justice in the land.' The Chief took a long drink of his coffee.

'And what have you been doing about Miss Jordan?' Foster continued with heat. 'Going over to Orchard House and making some kind of allegations there? Have you any idea of the damage you may have done her? Or me? I shall take this matter further, you can be very sure of that.'

Kelsey picked up a sugary biscuit, looked at it critically

and took a bite. 'Miss Jordan is looking for a business of her own,' he said mildly. 'She wants to buy one. Does that ring a bell with you?'

Foster was brought up short. 'Of course it does,' he said after a moment. 'I'm lending her the bulk of the capital to buy the business — when she finds it. Are you trying to make something out of that?'

Kelsey took another reflective bite. 'Are you in the habit,' he said, 'of making substantial loans on the strength of a brief acquaintance?'

Foster gave a long sigh. He dropped back into his chair and took a drink of coffee. 'Look here, Chief Inspector,' he said in the tone of a man striving to let the light of reason shine upon the conversation, 'I don't know what kind of farrago you've got in your head. The simple facts are these: My wife took a fancy to Miss Jordan, she was pleased with her, grateful to her. She greatly admired her skill in needlework. My wife was very fond of pretty clothes, fine materials, all that sort of thing.

'Miss Jordan told my wife in the course of conversation that she'd always wanted a business of her own but she lacked capital. My wife was very interested. She'd been looking for a new outlet, some hobby that would take her out a bit more, give her something fresh to think about. She told me she'd like to help Miss Jordan. She wanted some say in the business, of course.

'I gave a good deal of thought to the matter. My wife wasn't asking me for the money, she had her own money — it was my opinion she wanted. Miss Jordan struck me as very competent and even I could see her needlework was first-class.

'I agreed to what Vera asked. Everything would have to be gone into, of course, properly arranged. Vera told Miss Jordan she could go ahead, set the ball rolling.'

He paused and put his head in his hands. He was silent for a few seconds, then he sat up and took another drink of coffee. 'After my wife died, when Miss Jordan was leaving, she said to me: Am I to take it the loan is no longer on? I couldn't think what she meant, it had all gone out of my head. When I realized what she was talking about I told her: That's all right, you can go ahead, Vera would have wanted it.'

He looked at Kelsey. 'It's a perfectly sound business proposition, open to any kind of inspection. It isn't at variance with the general business practice of Cannonbridge Thrift.' He sounded flat and tired. 'If you'd asked me about it before I'd have told you what I've told you now, it never occurred to me to mention it.' He drained his coffee and poured himself another cup. Then he recollected himself and glanced about, offering more coffee, but there were no takers.

'I still can't see that it's any concern of yours,' he added in a tone that still strove to remain reasonable.

Let's get out of here, Sergeant Lambert said in his head, directing a fierce stream of thought at Kelsey. Let's gather ourselves up and retreat in as good order as possible.

As if in response Kelsey stood up. Lambert rose at once to his feet with a deep inward sigh of relief.

'Thank you for answering my questions so fully and patiently,' Kelsey said to Foster. 'I very much regret any distress I may have caused. We don't always relish the course on which we feel we must embark.'

Foster remained seated. He looked up at Kelsey and gave a brief nod. 'I understand,' he said. He gave a faint grin. 'One gets carried away at times.'

Kelsey didn't return the grin. He glanced at Miss Jordan who was sipping the last of her coffee. 'If you're ready, the least we can do is run you back to Orchard House.'

'That won't be necessary,' Foster put in. He looked across at Miss Jordan. 'Now that you're here we may as

well discuss the loan in more detail. I'll run you back to
Orchard House myself. I won't keep you long; fifteen,
twenty minutes.'

'Another twenty minutes won't make much difference,'
she said. 'They won't sack me over that.' She looked up at
the Chief. 'Thank you for the offer, but I'll go back with
Mr Foster.'

'I hope I haven't distressed you,' Kelsey said to her. 'Or
put you to too much inconvenience.'

She inclined her head by way of reply but her manner
remained detached and cool.

'We'll let ourselves out,' the Chief said to Foster. 'I'll
wish you both good day.'

As the sitting-room door closed behind them Lambert
heard the Chief let out a breath of relief. He slid Lambert
a sideways glance, rueful, touched with self-mockery.
'Let's get the hell out of here,' he said in an undertone.
The Chief's shoulders began to shake with silent laughter
as he felt the beginnings of a reaction.

Lambert followed him out into the fresh sweet air.
From the rear of the house he heard the click of a door
opening, the sound of voices, one of them Alma's, the
door closing again, the crunch of footsteps on the gravel
path.

Kelsey's shoulders continued to shake as they walked
down the drive to the car. Lambert glanced back and saw
Matt Bateman coming round the side of the house with
his easy swinging walk.

Kelsey's mood of laughter fell away, his shoulders
ceased to shake. 'If ever from this moment forward,' he
said to Lambert in a low voice full of subdued force, 'I
should grab you by the ear and tell you I've just had a
vision from heaven, a personal disclosure from the
Almighty that runs counter to all the evidence and all
known facts, tie me up and consign me to the cells until
I'm sane again.'

Lambert grinned. 'I'd like that in writing, signed and witnessed.'

Kelsey paused, looked at Lambert and gave an exaggerated shudder. 'For a moment back there I thought he'd decided to sue me. Or ring up the Chief Constable.' He closed his eyes briefly. 'Let this be a lesson to me. For ever and ever. Amen.' He turned his head and stood watching Matt Bateman coming towards them. 'I wish I felt as carefree as he looks,' he said. 'Not a worry in the world.' He raised his hand and called out, 'Hello there. Been passing the time of day with your niece? All right for some.'

Matt grinned as he came up to them. Under one arm he carried a tin that had once held biscuits. He gave it a pleased tap. 'Good cook, my Alma. No one to touch her for fruit-cake. Looks after her old uncle.'

His expression changed to one of sadness. 'Terrible business about poor Miss Vera.' He glanced from the Chief to Lambert. 'Knew her since she was a baby, from the day she was born, you might say.'

He glanced round at the garden. 'Used to do a couple of hours' work now and again for her Dad.' He shook his head sorrowfully. 'One of the old school, he was.' He glanced round at the shrubbery, at a neat stack of wood destined for the hearth in old Ned Pritchard's cottage. 'Always used to let me have my perks, Mr Murdoch. Used to let me have all the wood.'

Kelsey glanced at his watch and turned to the car.

'I always liked Miss Vera,' Matt said. 'Terrible to think how depressed she must have been, taking her life the way she did.' He adjusted the tin beneath his arm. 'And to think I saw her do it. In a manner of speaking.'

CHAPTER 17

Kelsey stood with his fingers on the handle of the car door. He felt his heart begin to thump in his chest.

'I must have seen her,' Matt said. 'More or less.'

'Surely not,' Sergeant Lambert said in an idle, rallying tone.

'That must have been what she was doing,' Matt said stoutly. 'Stands to reason. I saw the lights go on.'

'Oh yes?' Lambert allowed scepticism to colour his tone.

'It was all dark,' Matt said with protest. 'Not a light on anywhere. I was on my way home, walking along the top field. You can see Lynwood all the way along from there, you're looking at it across the dip. It's the only house in this stretch, you can't mistake it.

'I saw the lights go on. One after the other. It took me quite a time to walk along, the lights stayed on pretty well all that time.' Yes, Lambert thought, you couldn't get up much of a gallop, not with a bag full of pheasants.

'I thought nothing of it at the time,' Matt said. 'I knew Miss Vera was poorly, I just thought, poor soul, I expect she's having a bit of a wander round, restless like, getting herself a drink or something to read. I don't know what it is to lie awake myself, but it must be wearisome. Not natural. The good Lord meant us to work by day and sleep by night.'

And did the good Lord mean us to go poaching by night in Farmer Jauncey's top fields? Lambert said inside his head. That's what you were doing, my lad, up there in the silent hours.

But he didn't voice his thoughts, didn't let them move across his face.

The Chief remained looking down at his own fingers resting on the door handle. A turn of the head, a movement of the shoulders, the Chief Inspector displaying an interest in his movements that night and Matt would have recollected himself, forgotten his momentary desire for importance, would have been off like a risen bird.

'Afterwards,' he said earnestly, 'when I heard she'd killed herself—of course it wasn't really all that much of a surprise, we all knew she'd tried it once before, years ago—' He stopped and frowned, lost the thread of his thoughts.

'The lights,' Lambert prompted.

'Oh yes, the lights. Well, when I heard Miss Vera had died, I remembered seeing the lights. I thought to myself, Well, I never, that must have been when she did it.'

Lambert had a strong impulse to say: But she did it about ten o'clock and I'll bet my boots it was more like one in the morning when you were walking along the top field. But he held his peace.

'If only I'd known what she was doing,' Matt said. 'I could have run up to the house and banged on the door, wakened that Miss Jordan and got her to let me in. I could have run upstairs and smashed Miss Vera's door down. We could have saved her, like they did before.' He let out a long noisy breath.

'You didn't go to the inquest?' Lambert asked in a tone of mild interest. 'You didn't hear the evidence?'

'Not me. Can't abide such places.'

'I don't blame you,' Lambert said. 'Best plan is to stop at home. Out of harm's way. I don't suppose you read the papers either.'

'Papers!' Matt said with contempt. 'Waste of good money.' Even if you could manage to spell out more than the headlines, Lambert thought, which I'm prepared to wager you can't.

Lambert put a hand up to his mouth in a manufactured yawn. 'You could swear to what you've just told us?'

'Swear to it?' Matt said with a note of alarm. 'What do you mean—swear to it?'

'I just want to know,' Lambert said, light and easy, 'if you could swear to it if you had to. You're not just having us on?'

'But why? Where?' Matt said in a tone of incipient terror.

'Never mind where or why.' Lambert gave a half laugh. 'Could you swear to it? It's not just a leg-pull?'

'I don't know as I could.' Matt rolled his eyes like a startled horse as it dawned on him exactly what he'd told the Chief Inspector—that he was out of his bed and abroad at a time when honest citizens were sound asleep.

'I just went up to the top field for a bit of wood,' he said. 'That was all. I needed a bit of firewood. I don't usually go for wood in the dark but I'd run out. I did ask Mr Foster here if I could have some, there was a lovely little stack of wood by the shrubbery, but he wouldn't let me have it. Said he'd promised it to Ned Pritchard.' All the time he talked Matt looked nervously about, seeing the doors of the Cannonbridge courthouse gaping wide.

'No need to worry,' Kelsey said soothingly, still not turning round. 'I quite understand. Bit tricky saying where you were and what you were doing that time of night.' Snapping pheasants off trees with a wire, my lad, that's what you were up to, he added in his thoughts. You went up to the top field for wood earlier, in the daylight, you saw the pheasant droppings under the trees, decided to slip back again in the dark and snap them off as they roosted. Been a country lad in his time, had Kelsey, knew a thing or two about poaching. He half-turned, half-smiled at Matt. 'Carrying a bag full of feathers, were you?'

'I never said nothing about that,' Matt said in alarm.

'No, and maybe you won't need to. I dare say we

needn't ask too many questions about that. Not this time, anyway. I want you to tell me again about the lights. Exactly what you saw.'

Matt drew a long breath of relief. 'I saw the lights go on—'

'Which lights? How many? In what order?'

Matt half closed his eyes, looking back at that night, reading off the sequence photographed on his memory. 'There were three or four lights. The first one to come on was at the back on the first floor, a bedroom, that would be. Then another light near that, and then the lights in Miss Vera's room at the front. Then after a bit some more lights, the stairs and the kitchen, I reckon they'd be. They all stayed on together, then they started going out again, one by one. First the kitchen light, then the stairs. The last one to go out was the back bedroom. That just left Miss Vera's lights. They stayed on all the time I could see the house, I never saw them go off.'

'How long did all this take?'

'Ten minutes, fifteen, maybe a bit more.' Yes, Kelsey thought, take you all of that carrying a heavy bag of pheasants from the top of Jauncey's field, along the ridge.

'You'd swear to all this?'

Matt's eyes slid warily from Kelsey to Lambert. The sergeant gave him a friendly, encouraging grin. 'Well, yes, I suppose I could,' Matt said reluctantly. 'Though I don't understand—'

'Just technical detail,' the Chief said with massive reassurance. He was now fully turned towards Matt, he smiled on him with the full open countenance of authority in its most benign and unfrightening mood. 'Got to get the details correct, that's always of the greatest importance.'

'I dare say it is,' Matt said on a baffled note.

'And the time,' Kelsey said. 'The time you saw the lights go on?'

'I can tell you that well enough,' he said at once. 'It was gone half past two but not near three o'clock. It was ten minutes to three by my old grandfather clock in the kitchen when I got home.'

'Did you mention any of this to your niece? Alma Driscoll?'

'Not I!' Matt said at once. 'She'd have my guts.'

'Quite right too,' Kelsey said. 'You pay attention to Alma, you won't go far wrong.'

The Chief turned back towards the house. 'We'll just stroll back,' he said. 'We'll step inside for a moment.'

Lambert slipped an arm under Matt's elbow in a touch of gossamer steel. He exerted a light but compelling pressure which steered Matt along the drive. 'No need to alarm yourself,' he said.

They reached the house, mounted the steps. This time the Chief didn't press the bell. He opened the front door and went straight inside, along the hall. He opened the door leading into the sitting-room. The other two followed him.

The occupants of the room glanced up at them in surprise. Alma was standing beside Miss Jordan's chair, picking up her empty cup to place on her tray. Miss Jordan was still seated, she was reaching out to put a plate on the tray. Across the room Foster sat drinking yet another cup of coffee. All three of them remained motionless, staring.

When Matt saw Alma he almost turned and fled. The police might be willing this once to overlook his poaching—but Alma was another matter altogether. When she heard what he'd been up to—

She gave her uncle a look of piercing enquiry. He shook his head and pulled down the corners of his mouth to indicate ignorance and non-complicity in anything that was going forward.

'What's all this?' Foster asked abruptly, setting down his cup.

'Something I wish you to hear,' the Chief said. He turned to Matt. 'I want you to repeat what you told us out there.'

Alma gazed at Matt with a gathering frown. He avoided her eyes and went through his story again. No one moved or spoke as he recited the litany of the lights going on and off. 'Miss Vera's lights stayed on,' he ended. 'When all the other lights were out, hers were still on.'

There was a brief silence. Then Alma said on a loud high note, 'Three o'clock!' She turned on Miss Jordan a fierce, appalled look, she made a sudden movement towards her.

Miss Jordan glanced up at her with a blind gaze. Lambert reached out and put a hand on Alma's arm. She dropped into a chair and began to cry.

Matt said in nervous agitation, 'What's up? What's it all about?' No one heeded him.

'At half past two in the morning,' Kelsey said to Miss Jordan, 'Mrs Foster was indisputably dead. You were alone in the house. There was no other person to turn on the lights.' She made no answer. 'Did you turn on those lights?' he persisted with relentless civility.

She looked down at her hands. 'I woke up,' she said in a detached conversational tone. 'I was cold. I went down to the kitchen to make a hot-water bottle.'

'And in order to do that,' Kelsey said with the same insistence, 'you first went into Mrs Foster's bedroom?'

'I just looked in for a moment to see if she was all right.'

'And to do that you switched on all the lights in her room? Then you went off again, leaving all the lights on, locking her door behind you? If you looked in to see how she was, then you found she was dead. But you decided not to bother about that, you decided to lock her door and go downstairs, make yourself a nice hot-water bottle and then go back to bed and sleep soundly till morning.'

There was another silence, broken by Alma's sobs. 'You

told me earlier this morning,' Kelsey said to Miss Jordan, 'that you went to bed early that night, you slept heavily till morning, you heard nothing, weren't in any way disturbed, nothing woke you. Now you tell me you were walking about, upstairs and down, switching lights on and off, making hot-water bottles, looking into Mrs Foster's bedroom.'

She sat like an image carved from stone. Foster lifted the spoon from his saucer and moved it slowly between his fingers, studying it with care.

'I'll tell you what you did,' Kelsey said. 'You gave Mrs Foster a lethal dose of tablets in her chocolate at about ten o'clock. Shortly after that Mrs Foster switched off her light and went to sleep. Some hours later, at about half past two, when you were certain she was dead, you went along to her room. You were able to move freely about the house, there was no one else there. You opened doors and switched on lights as you pleased. You arranged the body to look like suicide, you did what was necessary with the keys, the radio, locking the doors, leaving the lights on.' Miss Jordan still said nothing. Foster continued to study his spoon, frowning in concentration.

'Was there any question,' Kelsey said suddenly, 'of marriage between you and Foster?'

She flashed the Chief a single upward glance, surprised, tinged with amusement. Foster said nothing, ceaselessly turning the spoon.

'Just the money then,' Kelsey said. 'A straightforward business deal. Hired for reward. Hired to kill Mrs Foster.' She made no response. Neither she nor Foster so much as glanced at each other.

'You had an extra key to the bedroom door,' Kelsey said. 'Given to you by Foster.' She made no reply.

Kelsey drew a long breath. 'I must ask you both to come down to the station. You'll both be charged.'

Alma stopped sobbing. She got to her feet and stood

looking down at Miss Jordan. 'I hope you rot in hell,' she said with violent force. 'What did she ever do to you?' Her face was distorted. A thick tress of hair fell forward across her cheek. Lambert put out a hand and drew her away.

Foster flicked a glance at Kelsey, then he looked down again, continued to toy with his spoon.

'I underrated you,' he said, watching his moving fingers. He began to smile with deep amusement. He looked across at Matt Bateman standing with a look of bafflement and horror on his face. 'I should have let you have that wood,' Foster said. He began to laugh.

His shoulders shook, he threw back his head and laughed aloud. His laughter turned suddenly to violent coughing. He picked up his cup and took a long drink of the cool coffee. He began to splutter and the coughing fit came back, he leaned forward, coughing and spluttering.

He pulled out a handkerchief, let out a long breath and dabbed at his mouth.

A thought flared in Kelsey's brain. He uttered an exclamation and sprang forward. Lambert grabbed at Edith Jordan's arm. She didn't resist, she made no move, intended none. She looked across at Foster, she drew a little shuddering breath and closed her eyes.

Kelsey reached Foster's side but Foster's hand had already fallen away from his mouth. The bitter-almond smell rose up at Kelsey. Foster glanced up at him with a look of triumph and sardonic amusement, a kind of bright mischief.

But it took him more than a minute to die and in that eternity of time the expression on his face underwent considerable change.

NOW READ ON WITH KEYHOLE CRIME

Other titles available in the shops now

THE TWELVE DEATHS OF CHRISTMAS
Marian Babson
MOTIVE IN SHADOW   *Lesley Egan*
CHILL FACTOR   *Aaron Marc Stein*
FATAL SWITCH   *Ian Stuart*
DEATH IN A COLD CLIMATE   *Robert Barnard*
DON'T OPEN THE DOOR   *Ursula Curtiss*
THE BEADED BANANA   *Margaret Scherf*
DEATH IS A DRUM . . . BEATING FOREVER
John Wyllie
THE BEAUTIFUL GOLDEN FRAME
Peter Chambers
STAR TRAP   *Simon Brett*
THE FAMILY VAULT   *Charlotte Macleod*
EXTRA KILL   *Dell Shannon*
EXPENDABLE   *Willo Davis Roberts*
NOWHERE?   *Aaron Marc Stein*
DEATH IN THE ROUND   *Anne Morice*
THE CHIEF INSPECTOR'S DAUGHTER
Sheila Radley

Look out for them wherever you normally buy paperbacks

 Keyhole Crime

OUR RECORD OF PREVIOUS CRIMES

Some of the exciting tales of murder, mystery, danger, detection and suspense already published in Keyhole Crime.

Look out for them wherever you normally buy paperbacks

 Keyhole Crime

A FEW CLUES ABOUT MORE GREAT TITLES YOU'LL SOON BE SEEING IN KEYHOLE CRIME

Dead dog
Charlaine Harris

'Introducing an author of rare talents...'
Publishers Weekly

It was already stiff, the legs poker straight in rigor mortis. It was covered in the fine powdery dust thrown up by every passing vehicle from the dirt road...
Catherine was used to flies buzzing and whining around her in the sizzling heat — they were unpleasant enough round a dead dog but far worse round the dead body she discovered in the old shack... Could this new death be related to the recent murder of her parents? Was theirs, in turn, the forerunner of a bizarre and frightening future that forced Catherine to suspect the people she had known all her life?

 Keyhole Crime

A FEW CLUES ABOUT MORE GREAT TITLES YOU'LL SOON BE SEEING IN KEYHOLE CRIME

DIG A LITTLE DEEPER

Ursula Curtiss

'First-rate fireside entertainment'
Sunday Times

'Gripping, well-written'
South Wales Argus

Lydia goes back to Connecticut for her cousin's wedding and has promised a friend that, while there, she will deliver a present to a Paula Blake who apparently lives down the road.
But her visit to the Blakes turns out to be vaguely unpleasant and, when an old lady suddenly dies, the tranquil country atmosphere takes on a subtle menacing edge and Lydia is uneasily surrounded by a mist of mystery…

 Keyhole Crime

A FEW CLUES ABOUT MORE GREAT TITLES YOU'LL SOON BE SEEING IN KEYHOLE CRIME

CAST, IN ORDER OF DISAPPEARANCE

Simon Brett

'Ingenious puzzle'
The Times

A somewhat unusual mystery in which Charles Paris discovers that the best time to stop a murder is before the victim is born.

As a bit-part actor with a taste for Scotch, girls and intrigue, Charles finds it easy to impersonate a policeman in order to help a pregnant showgirl. But what begins as a simple favour becomes a dangerous plot as the theatrical sleuth gets involved in a backstage drama of blackmail and murder, and plays a walk-on part in a monster movie with real blood. His.

 Keyhole Crime